Mills & Boon
Best Seller Romance

A chance to read and collect some of the best-loved novels from Mills & Boon—the world's largest publisher of romantic fiction.

Every month, four titles by favourite Mills & Boon authors will be re-published in the *Best Seller Romance* series.

A list of other titles in the *Best Seller Romance* series can be found at the end of this book.

Anne Hampson

UNWARY HEART

MILLS & BOON LIMITED
LONDON · TORONTO

All the characters in this book have no existence outside the imagination of the Author, and have no relation whatsoever to anyone bearing the same name or names. They are not even distantly inspired by any individual known or unknown to the Author, and all the incidents are pure invention.

The text of this publication or any part thereof may not be reproduced or transmitted in any form or by any means, electronic or mechanical, including photocopying, recording, storage in an information retrieval system, or otherwise, without the written permission of the publisher.

This book is sold subject to the condition that it shall not, by way of trade or otherwise, be lent, resold, hired out or otherwise circulated without the prior consent of the publisher in any form of binding or cover other than that in which it is published and without a similar condition including this condition being imposed on the subsequent purchaser.

First published 1969
Australian copyright 1981
Philippine copyright 1981
This edition 1981

© Harlequin Enterprises B.V. 1969

ISBN 0 263 73750 0

Set in Linotype Plantin 11 on 11½ pt.

*Made and printed in Great Britain by
Richard Clay (The Chaucer Press) Ltd,
Bungay, Suffolk*

CHAPTER ONE

MURIEL PATERSON met Andrew Burke less than four hours after the ship had left Southampton Docks, and that, she wrote and told her beautiful and sophisticated cousin, Christine, was the greatest piece of luck that had ever come her way. For Muriel's one ambition was to find a rich husband, and Andrew Burke was rich beyond her wildest dreams.

Of course, the opportunity would never have arisen if Aunt Edith, disappointed at the last moment by the friend who was to have accompanied her on the cruise, had not invited Muriel to take her place.

Aunt Edith was wealthy; she was also very mean, and therefore her offer had caused quite a stir in the Paterson household.

'It seems like providence,' said Mrs. Paterson on recovering from her surprise. 'This is the chance you've been waiting for, Muriel. Make the most of it, my dear, for you may never have another. Remember what I've told you – don't ruin your life as I did. When it comes to such an important business as marriage the head must rule the heart.'

For years this had been drilled into Muriel, but, being of a romantic disposition, she had secretly cherished other ideas concerning marriage ... until the last few months.

Her sister, Hilda – Dil as she was called by the family – had been married a mere six months, yet she and her husband quarrelled even more frequently than her parents.

'What did I tell you?' Mrs. Paterson would say with

boring reiteration. 'There's no happiness without money. I can only hope Muriel will have more sense than either of us.' And the last of Muriel's illusions was shattered the day Dil and Fred quarrelled over the baby.

'To quarrel over a baby! Oh, it's dreadful! You should both be so happy,' she told her sister who, white with anger, was hurling bitter imputations at her equally wrathful husband. Muriel's voice had been agonized and pleading as she tried to bring peace between them, but for all the notice they took of her she might have been dumb.

'If this hadn't happened I could have kept on with my work and we'd soon have saved up for a house of our own. Now, I suppose, we'll have to live with Mum and Dad for ever!'

'Shut up!'

'Dil – Fred— You used to be so happy.' Muriel glanced imploringly from one to the other. 'You were so in love – don't spoil it.'

'Love!' scoffed Dil. 'There's no such thing!'

Dil had ended up in tears and Muriel, unable to bear it any longer, fled to her room. Her sister was right; there was no such thing as love. She recalled that all her parents' disagreements were over the question of money. Money must be the all-important thing, for where there was lack of it even babies were not wanted. If she had money, thought Muriel, staring down at the grey, drab street below, she could help them to buy a house. She could also make sure her young brother realized his ambition, and she could buy her father a new van.

And so she had taken her mother's advice and paid a visit to her cousin, her worldly cousin who had once said,

'That face can buy you a rich husband, Muriel.

You'll be a fool if you don't exploit your looks.'

Christine had been delighted, and very optimistic.

'You may not meet enormously wealthy people on a short cruise like that,' she warned. 'But you will meet people who are much better off than you. The old girl's booked first, I suppose? She's a miserable skinflint at home, but she does like comfort when she's away.'

'We're going first class, yes.' Muriel paused. 'Aunt Edith has met very wealthy people on her cruises; people who are even as rich as she. Once she received a Christmas card from a real lord she'd met on a cruise.'

'Real lords aren't always wealthy.' Christine smiled faintly at her cousin's surprise. 'So watch your step. And now for the tips you want, darling. First, you must have glamour, and plenty of it. Just look what glamour's done for me.' It had brought her four proposals of marriage in as many months, she went on to inform her cousin proudly, and added,

'But I want money and love. You, of course, can't afford to be so particular – you haven't a father who's the richest man in Barston.'

They went up to Christine's lovely bedroom; the dressing-table was littered with bottles and jars.... The 'groom' course had begun.

Christine showed her how to use cosmetics to the best advantage, how to do her hair and, in a sudden burst of generosity, gave her two evening gowns which, so she said, would do the trick. The dresses, although unmistakably expensive, were incredibly low-cut, and they seemed garish beside the demure little creation Muriel's father had recently bought for her nineteenth birthday. Muriel suppressed a shudder; they must be all right if Christine wore them. 'I'm old-fashioned,' she thought, and gave her whole attention to what her cousin was saying.

'Men always become romantic in the evenings – and by the way, don't, for heaven's sake, mention that you serve in your father's greengrocer's shop.'

'But if I do meet someone he'll be bound to find out.'

'Later, yes, but it won't matter once he's fallen in love with you. No, darling, do try to hide your poverty.'

'But I can't say I'm rich, Christine.'

'I'm not asking you to,' she returned impatiently. 'Simply try to hide the fact that you're so poor, that's all. My clothes will help.'

'Very well,' said Muriel, beginning to feel some anxiety about the success of her scheme.

She listened attentively to the voice of experience, making mental notes of all she must and must not do. Christine lent her an evening wrap, sportswear and dresses which all seemed far too loud and daring.

'You can have this perfume – this for the daytime, and this for the evening. You'll be surprised what perfume can do,' Christine told her, a knowing look in her eyes. 'It just goes to a man's head.'

Trying on one of the evening gowns, Muriel gasped at her reflection as she stood before the mirror.

'It doesn't look like me at all.' She shuddered. 'If I marry a rich man will I have to look like this all the time? – and have all this horrid stuff on my face?'

'You will become so used to it you'll feel undressed without it,' laughed Christine, glancing at her cousin in admiration.

'I don't think I could stand it,' protested Muriel, almost ready now to drop the whole idea.

'Don't be silly.' Christine's voice was sharp. 'Rich men want glamour, I've proved it. That little girl look of yours is quite out of date, and so is your naïve manner of speaking. You must try to copy me – be worldly, confident, and remember that you're very beautiful.'

Muriel wrinkled her nose; she felt sticky and her mouth looked too big. As for her hair! It certainly made her appear sophisticated, piled on top of her head like that, but to Muriel's critical gaze it looked ridiculous. Tentatively she mentioned this to her admiring cousin.

'Nonsense, Muriel. You're far too old-fashioned.'

'I suppose you're right.' Muriel sighed and glanced again at her reflection. The word 'wanton' seemed to be splashed across the mirror, and she had to smile to herself. Christine dressed like this, and she never looked a wanton.

'You must learn to make play with your eyes; men fall for that – they're too stupid to know what you're about. No, don't walk like that – like this . . . no, darling, your hair won't fall down. Leave it alone . . . don't wrinkle your forehead, it makes you look childish. . . .' And so it had continued until Christine was perfectly satisfied. 'Now it's up to you, and the best of luck. Go all out to get your man.'

'Y – yes,' returned Muriel vaguely.

'And don't forget to write to let me know how things are going.'

To Christine's disgust Muriel insisted on letting her hair down and washing her face before going home.

'Your mother wouldn't have known you,' Christine said.

No, and neither would her father, thought Muriel, trembling at the very idea of his seeing her with so much heavy make-up on her face.

Her aunt had invited her to stay the night, but knowing her father could not put up the orders alone in the morning, she refused.

'The first bus from here isn't until nine,' she said, 'and Daddy has to be out by then.'

'How will he manage while you're away?' her aunt inquired, without much interest.

'Mother's going to the shop every day.'

'She won't like that,' her aunt returned grimly.

'The round is the worst job,' Muriel retorted and, after a slight hesitation, 'but if I do find a rich husband—' how dreadful that sounded! – 'I shall buy him a new van. The one we have now is so old that it keeps on letting him down.'

'You still have that old contraption he bought at first?'

'We can't afford another; they're so terribly dear.'

'I'd hate to be so poor,' interposed Christine with a shudder as she watched her mother pouring tea from an exquisite Georgian silver teapot. 'It must be awful for Aunt Emily after what she was used to as a girl.'

'Entirely her own fault; she wouldn't listen to advice. There were four sisters of us and she was the only one to marry beneath her. I'm relieved to find you don't intend to spoil your life, Muriel.'

'I love my father,' she flashed, 'and I won't have him spoken of in that disparaging manner! The trouble is, only I understand him. He's so gentle and kind, and he sacrifices himself for us all the time.'

'My dear, I admire your loyalty, but I still say your mother ought never to have married him. Just think what a difference it would have made to you children if she'd married someone of her own class – oh, I know he managed to let you and Dil stay on at school, but what good has it done you? And although Derek is safely at the grammar school I doubt very much if your father will afford to let him go on to university. When he's sixteen he'll probably have to leave school and find work.'

'He won't.' Muriel's hands clasped under the table. 'He wants to go in for law.'

Aunt Sarah shook her head.

'What he wants and what your father will be able to afford are two different things. You say your father is not in the best of health, so it's more than likely that Derek will have to go into the shop, unless,' she added significantly, 'you happen to be in a position to help.'

Muriel flushed. So much depended on her, and the success of the forthcoming trip. And yet she suddenly faltered. Could she change her whole personality? – put aside for ever all that had so endeared her to her father?

Watching her niece across the table, Aunt Sarah thought she had never seen a lovelier girl. Of medium height, Muriel was slender and graceful with grey green eyes and chestnut hair. Nature had deftly blended delicacy with character to create a face of unusual beauty. The girl would be a fool not to exploit those looks to the full.

'I sincerely hope I shall be in that position,' said Muriel with grim resolve.

And so it was the mercenary, sophisticated Muriel Paterson who boarded the *Appenia* one week later.

Her aunt went straight to her cabin; Muriel, to whom every small incident was a novelty, stayed by the rail until the ship was clear of the docks. Then she made her way to the main stairs. Descending them, she became confused, but one of the ship's officers made a timely appearance and within a few minutes she was in her aunt's cabin.

The old lady was lying on the bed.

'Go away,' she snapped irritably. 'I'm about to be frightfully ill.'

'We've only just sailed.' Muriel looked at her blankly. 'How do you know you're going to be ill?'

'Because I'm always ill for the first couple of days,' she grumbled. 'It's such a waste when I can't take the meals.'

Muriel had to smile; Aunt Edith hated waste of any kind.

'Shall I come back later?'

'You can if you like, but I warn you, I'm not a pretty sight when I'm ill.'

Muriel's cabin, although first class, had no verandah like her aunt's, but it did have a private bath, and within half an hour she was sitting before the mirror surveying herself with relief, and grimacing at the recollection of the shock she had given her aunt. But she dismissed it from her mind, refusing to dwell on those scathing and denunciatory remarks.

All the same, it was a pity rich men had to have glamour, she thought, picking up a comb and running it through her hair. Again she faltered, then before her rose the vision of her father. How pale and tired he had begun to look, and what an effort it was these days for him to lift the heavy sacks of vegetables and boxes of fruit. And he always seemed so fatigued when he returned from the round ... Muriel's lips set in a grim, determined line and she proceeded to apply her 'glamour' according to her cousin's instructions.

Just before dinner she returned to her aunt's cabin; the old lady was still lying on the bed looking exceedingly sorry for herself.

'Aren't you coming to dinner?' Muriel began hesitantly.

'Do I look as though I could eat dinner!' She did seem rather pasty, Muriel realized, but she refrained from saying so. 'If I could eat my dinner you can be sure I'd do so—— What on earth have you got on?' She sat bolt upright and propped a pillow behind her lace-capped head. 'I'd never have brought you if I'd known you were going to get yourself up like this. That dress is positively indecent! Strapless, do they call them? More like topless, I should say!'

'Everyone wears low-cut dresses these days,' Muriel protested, though she did go slightly red.

'Well, they don't suit you. And if you think that stuff improves your face then you're a fool! And that hair – rich husband, indeed! You're enough to frighten any man away, any decent man, that is. But I don't suppose you care so long as he's got money. Who put this idea into your head, anyway? Sit down and tell me!'

Muriel sat down meekly – one always felt meek in Aunt Edith's presence – and told her about Fred and Dil, saying she was sure they would not quarrel so if only they had a house of their own. She hadn't got far, however, when her aunt interrupted her.

'They must be happy; they've only been married a few months.'

'They are not, Aunt Edith; they quarrel shockingly. It always starts over the baby now——'

'Baby? What baby?'

'Dil's baby – she hasn't got it yet,' she added hastily. 'But she blames Fred for it. You see, if she wasn't having it she'd still be working and then they could save up for a house.'

'I don't see how all this concerns you.'

'My family's happiness does concern me,' she said quietly.

'So you've decided to marry for money? Bosh! When you marry, my girl, it will be for love! You're made that way.'

'I thought so once,' Muriel confessed wistfully. 'But I've changed now. Look what good I could do if I had money. I could put everything right at home, and I might be able to put the deposit down for a house for Dil and Fred.'

'Why should you?' her aunt retorted. 'If Dil's made a mess of her life that's no reason why you should make a mess of yours in order to get her out of it.'

'There is Derek....'

Her aunt regarded her shrewdly.

'I suppose your mother thinks I could help?' Muriel flushed. Her family never had a good word for Aunt Edith, but Muriel could see her point of view. She had a daughter married to an American who was now living in Boston. She had three sons, and it was only natural that Aunt Edith should think of their future first. 'Well, I don't intend to,' the old lady went on. 'Your mother's a bad manager and I'm not giving her money to waste. She has a fine man and doesn't appreciate him.'

Muriel warmed to her; she was the only one of her relations who ever had a good word for her father. After a little while she rose, and her aunt, sniffing distastefully, exclaimed,

'What's that horrible smell?'

'It's – perfume. Christine gave it to me.'

'Christine? I didn't think you had anything to do with her!'

'I don't see her very often, but when I knew I was coming with you I went to see her – she lent me some clothes.'

'I see...' The old woman regarded her niece sternly and perceptively. 'So it was she who put you up to this? She gave you all the hints she knew on how to catch a man—'

'Aunt Edith!'

'I know Christine. You'll do well to keep away from that girl, she's a minx! I may be stuck away in the country, but I hear things. The latest is that she's got about half a dozen men dangling on her string. Can't see that their only interest is her father's money.'

'Oh, I'm sure it isn't that, Aunt Edith,' Muriel protested. 'Christine's very beautiful and talented. Also, she confided to me that she's no longer interested in men – what I mean is, she doesn't want them all running after her now, because she's met the man she intends to marry.'

'*She* intends to marry? That seems an odd way of putting it.'

Muriel laughed.

'Well, you see, Aunt Edith, he doesn't know anything about her falling in love with him because they've only met once. He's a business associate of Uncle Herbert's, and he's very rich and handsome,' she went on with a certain amount of awe. 'The only thing Christine doesn't like about him is that he has a very commanding personality, and she thinks he may be rather bossy. Apart from that Christine says he's absolutely perfect.'

'Rather bossy, eh? That won't suit my lady Christine at all. I hope she gets him, she needs a master, that one. Always had far too much of her own way. I warned Sarah, but she never took any heed.'

'Christine says she will soon curb this young man's arrogance once she gets to know him better.'

'Oh, she does, does she? Takes a whole lot too much for granted – always did! But one of these days that little minx will get a set-down. I've never liked her and if you were a child of mine I wouldn't allow you to have anything to do with her.'

'She is really very nice—'

'She's not! And if you take my advice you'll keep her at a distance, otherwise you're going to find yourself in some trouble. Ensnaring rich husbands may be the thing with women of her type, but it doesn't suit you; you're not cut out for a vixen. Enjoy yourself on this trip – heaven knows you get little enough pleasure stuck behind that counter all the time – but forget Christine and her advice on how to trap unsuspecting males.'

'But I *must* try. If I succeed I can make all the family happy – and myself,' she added as an afterthought, wondering why her tone lacked conviction. 'When you asked me to come with you it seemed a sort of – omen.'

'Rubbish! You watch out it doesn't prove to be a bad omen. Supposing you do trap some rich fool—'

'There's no question of trapping,' retorted Muriel indignantly. 'I only mean to do as Christine advised and leave the rest to – luck.'

'Never believed in luck myself,' her aunt grunted. 'Anyway, in spite of your denials it all boils down to deliberate man-hunting. Now, what if you do trap a man into marriage, have you considered what his reaction will be when he finds out?'

'Aunt Edith,' said Muriel patiently, 'I don't intend to trap anyone. I shall merely be pleasant and hope someone will be attracted to me.'

'In other words, you're selling your looks,' her aunt asserted bluntly, 'and you have a fortnight in which to do it. My dear girl, men are not fools; they don't run off and marry a girl they've known only two weeks.'

'I understand that,' she admitted, blushing furiously at her aunt's plain speaking. 'But if someone likes me enough he'll wish to continue our friendship.'

'You appear to have it all worked out to perfection,

but I can only hope, for your own sake, that you will fail in your endeavours.'

'You think that if I do succeed he will be sure to find out some time that I – deliberately tried to – to—'

' "Catch" is the word I think you prefer,' Aunt Edith put in smoothly, 'though I fail to see the difference.'

'He can't find out,' Muriel said, becoming hotter and hotter. 'How can he? Nobody knows except you and Christine and Aunt Sarah.'

'And your family, that makes—' Aunt Edith frowned. 'Does your father know about this?'

'No – we thought it best not to tell him,' Muriel confessed. 'He would never have let me come.'

'No, of course he wouldn't – I ought to have known he'd be in ignorance of all this.' She looked very worried. 'You must drop the whole idea, Muriel, do you hear me!' But before Muriel had time to reply she waved her away impatiently. 'Oh, dear,' she groaned. 'I feel terrible – no, don't fuss – go away.'

'Are you sure—?'

'*Go away!*'

In spite of her glamorous air and apparent sophistication Muriel felt very small and frightened as she entered the dining saloon, but she contrived to hide her nervousness as the table steward came forward to conduct her to the table at which were seated a middle-aged lady and gentleman. She sat down; was her dress really too low? she wondered, glancing at the couple to see what effect her appearance had on them. If they found anything unusual, however, they managed to hide it behind a polite smile, and within a few minutes they were chatting pleasantly to her.

'So this is your first cruise?' Mrs. Worsley said. 'We do one every year; in our opinion it's the ideal holiday –

if you like the sea, of course.'

'My aunt thinks so, too. She used to go twice a year when her husband was alive.'

Mr. Worsley, a short, jolly-faced man with thick white brows and a wrinkled forehead, glanced at the empty chair.

'Is your aunt with you, then?'

'Yes, but she's not very well. She is always ill for the first couple of days.'

'Lots of people are, but it doesn't stop them coming. You see the same people year after year, and it's amazing the friends you make. I've already seen four people I know.'

'You have?' His wife looked interested. 'Who are they?'

'Mr. and Mrs. Powell – I saw them as we were embarking, but I haven't seen them since – and those two young men who shared our car for the Naples trip last year. What are their names?' He shook his head. 'I can't remember, but there they are, over at the table in the corner.'

His wife, glancing over her shoulder, knitted her brows in concentration.

'One of them is called Andrew – I remember that because we have a son, Andrew,' she explained to Muriel, who wasn't very interested because she was studying the menu. She had a healthy appetite and such things as roast duckling and peaches in jelly made her feel quite hungry. 'I can't remember their surnames at all.'

Muriel thoroughly enjoyed her first dinner on board, feeling quite at home with her table companions who were rather typical of the more well-to-do of her father's customers. Mr. Worsley ordered wine and insisted on her taking a glass; she made sure to sip it slowly, not knowing what effect it might have on her.

'I suppose you're joining the dancers in the night club?' Mrs. Worsley spoke as though it were a foregone conclusion. 'I think we shall just sit and watch for a while and then turn in. I always seem to feel sleepy on my first evening at sea.'

Muriel thought it would be nice to stay with this homely couple, but of course they would not want her. Besides, she would stand a far better chance of meeting a young man if she went dancing, for despite her aunt's warnings, she meant to proceed with her plan. Looking round, however, she soon realized that most of the men were accompanied by ladies. This wasn't going to be as easy as she had imagined. Her courage began to ebb; she could never go dancing on her own.

'I think I'll go to my cabin and read,' she said flatly, and both her companions looked up in surprise.

'You can read at home,' Mr. Worsley exclaimed.

'I h-haven't a partner,' she stammered, flushing. 'I would rather go to my cabin.'

'I'm quite sure you wouldn't,' Mrs. Worsley returned emphatically. 'Henry, we must find Miss Paterson a partner.'

'Oh, no!' The very idea shocked Muriel and she realized she would never acquire the cool confidence of her cousin who would, no doubt, quite easily have found a partner for herself. Ignoring her protest, Mrs. Worsley told her husband to fetch the two young men over to their table.

'We are all one happy family on these cruises,' she informed Muriel with a smile. 'If you'd been before you would know that.' She went on to say what nice young men they were, all the while nodding and gesticulating in their direction.

'But I can't let you ask one of them to be my

partner.' Muriel's behaviour was in complete contrast to her appearance, and it seemed impossible that her plan could ever be carried out successfully. She wasn't clever enough; she just hadn't the nerve. . . .

'They're coming this way.' Having risen to do his wife's bidding, Mr. Worsley hesitated. 'They've recognized us.'

They certainly had, and there was nothing for Muriel to do but stay and be introduced to them. Both men were tall, but the dark one was slightly taller than the other and it was on him that Muriel's eyes were fixed. There was something lordly in the way he carried himself, and a certain dignified courtesy in his finely modulated voice when he addressed Mr. Worsley.

'I thought I saw you on deck before we sailed.' He gave Mrs. Worsley a most charming smile. 'How are you?'

'Fine, thanks – and you?'

'Quite well, thank you.'

While her husband went in search of another chair, Mrs. Worsley began the introductions.

'I'm so sorry,' she laughed, 'but I can remember only your first name, Mr. – Mr.—?'

'Burke – and this is Bill Raines.'

'Ah, yes, I remember now.' She introduced Muriel to them and when her husband arrived with the chair they all sat down.

Muriel liked Bill on sight, but she was not too sure about Andrew. He was talking to Mr. Worsley and she watched him unobserved for some moments. He had jet black hair which was inclined to wave, and dark features which, although undeniably handsome, portrayed both arrogance and ruthlessness. Her impression was that he would make a staunch and dependable friend, but an unmerciful enemy. So intently were her eyes fixed upon him that it was impossible for him not to sense her interest, and he turned a mild stare in her direction. Muriel blushed, and his brows lifted slightly, his expression changing to one of puzzlement. The blush appeared to puzzle him. Muriel sternly pulled herself together; it would be stupid to lose her poise at a time like this. Not that she thought of trying her luck on Andrew Burke, but there was his friend.

'This is Miss Paterson's first trip,' Mrs. Worsley was saying, 'and she's actually thinking of going to her cabin to read. What do you think of that, Mr. Burke?'

Andrew suppressed a yawn.

'I think it's an excellent idea,' he said. 'Bill has found a young lady he met on another trip and they're going dancing; I think I shall follow Miss Paterson's example.' His manner was distinctly cold – in fact, for some quite inexplicable reason, Muriel felt she'd been snubbed.

'Oh, how ungallant of you,' Mrs. Worsley chided. 'I was just going to ask you two to take Miss Paterson with you. I took it for granted you'd be going along to the night club.'

'We could make a foursome,' Bill suggested, and Andrew's brows lifted a little higher as he met his gaze. Then his eyes flickered again to Muriel; they held contempt, distaste ... but it was the sensation of being stripped that caused Muriel to squirm and brought the angry colour flooding to her cheeks.

'I would much rather go to my cabin,' she said with what dignity she could muster. That hateful man should not think her a suppliant craving for his company! 'But thank you all the same for wishing to find me a partner.'

Andrew's gaze took on a new interest and he appeared to be amused. His tone, however, was colourless when he spoke.

'I had no idea you were going to your cabin simply because you'd no partner,' he said. 'I shall be delighted to do as Mrs. Worsley suggests.

'I'm going to my cabin because I'm tired!' She hadn't meant to snap, but judging by the expressions on the faces of her companions she had undoubtedly displayed her temper. This seemed to add considerably to Andrew's amusement.

'I'm quite sure you're not tired,' he said laughingly. 'I shall take you dancing, Miss Paterson.' A distinct emphasis on the word 'shall', and it was with difficulty that Muriel controlled herself. She had no wish to offend her table companions, so she refused his offer graciously, saying she really was tired. Perhaps another evening. . . .

'Miss Paterson's a little embarrassed because I asked you to partner her,' interrupted Mrs. Worsley, 'but there's no need to be, my dear. Tell her, Mr. Burke, that we're just one free-and-easy, happy family on these trips.'

'Quite right,' Bill put in encouragingly. 'Do come and make a foursome, Miss Paterson.' His smile was charming; Andrew smiled, too, but Muriel sensed he was no longer amused. Mr. and Mrs. Worsley waited expectantly; Muriel felt that to continue her refusals would only result in her own discomfort.

'If you're sure you don't mind?' she began, looking at Andrew and wondering why she should suddenly feel so tensed and afraid, as though some terrible catastrophe were about to overtake her.

'As I said, Miss Paterson, I shall be delighted to take you dancing.'

The dancing began at nine o'clock and ended at midnight. Bill introduced Muriel to his friend, Kathleen, a fair-haired, vivacious girl who appeared to take an instant liking to her, and despite the bad beginning Muriel thoroughly enjoyed herself. Twice during the evening she slipped away to her aunt's cabin; the first time the old lady merely snapped, the second time she ordered Muriel out and told her not to return that evening.

When the dancing was over Bill and Kathleen said good night and went off by themselves. Muriel turned to her companion.

'Thank you very much,' she began, then pulled herself up, convinced that that wasn't quite the right thing to say.

'The pleasure was all mine,' Andrew returned in a soft, lazy drawl. 'Shall I see you to your cabin?'

Reaching it, he bade her good night.

'I hope your aunt will be better in the morning,' he added, making no arrangements for another meeting, and as she went slowly into her cabin and sat down at the dressing-table Muriel felt inexplicably flat and depressed.

'I wish he hadn't seen me like this—' Angrily she seized a pad of cotton wool and, dipping it into a jar of cleansing cream, removed the heavy make-up from her face.

Why had she said that?

She frowned at her reflection, could find no reason, and after a moment she turned her thoughts to other, more important matters.

Bill. . . . Pity he had found Kathleen; he would have done very well. Andrew. . . . No use wasting time on him; he was the stiff, unemotional type that never fell in love, the sort of man who would grow into a crusty old bachelor, long-haired and eccentric. Pity, though, for he appeared to be frightfully rich, for Bill had asked him how he was liking the new Bentley. . . . Muriel heaved a deep sigh; yes, it really was a pity.

But who else was there? Most of the men seemed to be married, or were in mixed parties. I think I'll have to drop the idea, she mused dejectedly. In any case, if I do find someone, I doubt if I could remain convincing for very long.

The trouble was – and it had happened twice this evening – she had a childish habit of exclaiming and clapping her hands when anything pleased or excited her. Andrew, she recalled, had frowned most oddly at her, and then his eyes had half closed, hiding his expression.

She let her hair fall on to her shoulders, gazing dreamily into the mirror. It *had* been wonderful dancing with Andrew, though – and what envious glances had been cast in her direction!

At last she undressed and slid between the cool sheets; but it was a long time before she slept. It would have been considerably longer had she overheard the conversation going on in the state-room where Andrew had been joined by Bill.

'You know, I was beginning to regret having let you persuade me to come on this trip – I was bored to death the last time – but now I believe it's going to be interesting.' Andrew poured himself a drink and sat down, an expression of faint contempt on his handsome face.

'The Paterson girl?' Bill glanced up wonderingly, his glass poised half-way to his lips. 'There's a much nicer one at the table next to ours – couldn't take her eyes off you at dinner.'

'Didn't notice her.'

'You must have. Red dress and blonde hair.'

'Oh, her? Pretty but uninteresting. Besides,' he added, 'I'm not in the habit of flirting with innocent little girls; they're apt to be hurt and, although you may be rather sceptical, I have a conscience.'

Bill laughed.

'The Paterson girl shouldn't give you any conscience trouble. I'll wager she knows all the rules.'

'Yes, indeed. The typical good-time girl with one object in view.' Andrew's mouth curved into an amused sneer. 'Haven't been dodging 'em for years without learning to spot them at a glance. Well, I'm very willing to play, so long as the game's played my way. That girl needs a lesson, and I decided to give her one when she pretended to be embarrassed by Mrs. Worsley's asking me to partner her.'

'Seemed more indignant than embarrassed, and that was because you'd already practically snubbed her.' Bill paused in thought, a slight frown appearing on his brow. 'I felt almost sorry for her; that's why I suggested taking her with us. I had the impression that she really meant what she said about preferring to go to her cabin.'

'Part of the act,' Andrew said with contempt. 'Those women all follow the same pattern, all display a marked reluctance at first, a lack of eagerness. You have no need to waste your pity on that girl. She asked to be introduced to us.'

'I can't see how you reached that conclusion,' his friend mildly protested. 'If she's fortune-hunting then her interest is in wealthy men, and how could she know we come into that category?'

'She can't know anything about any man until she has met him. As it happens, though, she'd been doing a little pumping. I saw Mrs. Worsley glance over in our direction several times as she talked to the girl; we were definitely under discussion, and if we hadn't gone over Mr. Worsley would have beckoned us. He was about to do so as we rose from our table.'

'But the Worsleys don't know much about us!'

'Enough. Last year, when old Worsley said he had shares in the Munro Electrical Company, you told him mine was the rival firm, remember?'

'Yes – yes, I do,' responded Bill thoughtfully, draining his glass, and then, 'What's your intention? Will you make her fall for you and then throw her over?'

'She's not the sort of woman who falls in love,' Andrew said with a sneer. 'No, I intend to convince her that she has me safely – er – hooked, and then....' He reached for his glass, his expression changing to one of amusement.

'And then...?' A sudden frown creased his friend's brow. 'Oh, leave the girl alone, Andrew!'

'Not likely; I intend to have some fun. As I said, that girl needs a lesson, and it so happens that I'm in the very mood to give her one.'

CHAPTER TWO

WHEN Muriel arrived at the swimming-pool the next morning she found her three companions of the previous evening already there. They were playing with an enormous rubber ball, and as it came out of the water and bounced at her feet Muriel picked it up and threw it back.

'Come on in,' Kathleen shouted. 'It's glorious!'

For half an hour they all played and swam together, and when they came out Andrew picked up Muriel's wrap and put it round her shoulders.

'Are you going to like your first cruise?' he asked, smiling down at her in his most charming manner.

'Yes, oh, yes, I'm sure I am,' she returned impulsively, forgetting her role for the moment. 'It's all so new and exciting.'

Andrew frowned, and took a good look at her. She seemed much younger in her swim-suit.... Not nearly as old as he had thought, and not so experienced, either. But she was doing very well, and she'd improve with practice. A touch of contempt curved his lips, to be replaced by a smile as Bill and Kathleen came up to them. They were laughing and obviously enjoyed each other's company very much indeed.

'We're coming again tonight,' Kathleen said, shaking out her curls, 'for a moonlight bathe. Are you two coming?'

Muriel looked up at Andrew, waiting breathlessly for his reply.

'Would you care to, Miss Paterson?'

'Yes, I'd love it. I've never been moonlight bathing before.'

'There's a first time for everything,' he said, and added, 'You swim remarkably well. Do you do much of it?'

'I used to, but our baths closed down and the nearest is ten miles away – at Barston.'

'Barston?' Bill shot Andrew a glance. 'You live ten miles from Barston?'

'Yes; do you know it?'

Andrew's eyes were narrowed. So she lived near Barston, did she?

'I live there,' Bill answered, glancing again at his friend. 'You must know Andrew's place, then?'

Muriel shook her head; Andrew watched her intently, his eyes still narrowed.

'No, I don't.' She stared. 'Burke and Groves ...? Is that you?'

How well she did it! He felt almost tempted to remind her that the Worsleys had already told her who he was, but that would spoil everything. She must not discover he was as clever as she – not yet.

'I am the first half,' he replied smoothly. 'It's a small world, Miss Paterson.'

Burke and Groves ... the large electrical works in the 'Park', Barston's great industrial centre, and employing thousands of men and women. ...

'Do you live in Barston, Mr. Burke?'

'I live thirty miles from Barston, in the country.' He then abruptly changed the subject and after arranging to meet on the sports deck after breakfast they went their separate ways.

When she had dressed Muriel went along to her aunt's cabin; the steward had brought fruit, but it lay untouched on the little chest by the bed.

'Are you worse, Aunt Edith?' she gasped in concern.

'Of course I'm worse,' snapped the old lady, thinking again of all the meals she was paying for and not eating. 'What are you gaping at? I know I'm white, but there's no need to stand there as if you'd seen a ghost!'

'Shouldn't you have the doctor?' Muriel began.

'I'm not paying for any doctor – don't believe in them, you know that. I've never had a doctor in my life and I don't intend starting now. Have you had your breakfast?'

'Not yet; I was just going, but I think I'll stay with you.'

'You will do nothing of the kind. It's enough for one of us to miss the meals. Run along, and don't come back till after lunch.'

'After lunch? Aunt Edith, you can't lie here all alone, and with nothing to – to—'

'If you mention food,' her aunt warned darkly, 'I'm liable to have another attack right now.' She waved a hand in dismissal. 'Go and get your breakfast – wait a moment. What are our table people like?'

'Very nice; a middle-aged couple and most friendly.'

'Good. Pleasant table companions can make such a difference to a cruise.' She paused, her pale eyes stern. 'I wonder what they thought of you in those disgusting clothes, and with all that rubbish on your face?'

'They didn't find anything unusual in my appearance,' Muriel replied stiffly. 'I'm only in the fashion.'

'Fashion, my foot; you looked ridiculous! But I suppose they were too polite to show any surprise. Did you take notice of what I said?'

Muriel flushed and hesitated for a moment.

'Mrs. Worsley introduced me to two gentlemen,' she began cautiously. 'And one of them is a partner in the firm of Burke and Groves in Barston – you know it, of course?'

'Barston?' She looked surprised, and then shrugged lightly. 'It's funny how one always seems to meet people from one's own part of the country on these cruises. Burke and Groves, did you say?' She broke of, eyeing her niece suspiciously. 'Did you vamp him?'

Really, Aunt Edith's lack of delicacy was outrageous, Muriel thought, her cheeks burning more hotly than ever.

'I did not, and I have no intention of vamping anyone. I wouldn't know how, anyway.'

'You said last night that that was your intention—'

'I didn't!' she protested indignantly. 'I said I intended to try to attract someone—'

'You'd have attracted someone a darned sight easier if you'd remained as you were,' her aunt told her scathingly. 'You look thirty and as worldly as a baggage.'

'I don't! You have no right to speak to me like this simply because I've acquired a little glamour. It's the fashion to be glamorous – look what it's done for Christine, she's had four proposals of marriage in four months. Men never even look at a girl who has no glamour – at least,' she amended knowledgeably, 'rich men don't.'

'You not only look like a baggage,' the old lady retorted, ignoring her protests, 'you also talk like one. Do you suppose this Burke fellow will fall for you? Is it Burke you've met?'

'Yes....' She stared musingly into space. 'I think he must like me, for he's arranged to meet me after breakfast. And this evening we're going moonlight bathing—'

'You're *what*?'

'Please, Aunt Edith, there's no need to look so shocked. Bill – that's the other young man – and his friend Kathleen suggested it, so there can't be anything unusual in it.'

But Aunt Edith, her ideas of propriety outraged, silenced her with an imperative wave of the hand.

'You're going on no moonlight bathing escapade,' she said inexorably, 'so you can get the idea right out of your head. You came on this trip as my companion and you'll stay here with me tonight.'

'But you said you didn't want me till you were better.' Muriel was almost in tears. 'You said you couldn't bear to have anyone with you when you were like this.'

'I've changed my mind. You'll stay and keep me company this evening; come straight here when you've had your dinner.'

There was no arguing with her. Besides, Muriel thought, she *had* come as her aunt's companion and therefore she'd never expected complete freedom on the cruise.

'Very well,' she said, her voice quivering with disappointment. 'Is there anything you want now?'

'No, go and get your breakfast.'

The orchestra was playing light music in the forward lounge; Muriel and Andrew, hot and tired after their game of deck tennis, sat down and relaxed while waiting for the others to join them. Then they all sipped iced lemonade and chatted. After a while Muriel said she would not be joining them that evening, after all.

'I thought your aunt preferred to be alone when she was ill?' Andrew was watching her curiously.

'She did want to be alone last night – but she wants me with her this evening.' Muriel realized that she ought not to have used the word 'want'; it seemed to reveal everything. Andrew's expression strengthened the idea; he appeared to have reached a conclusion. Had he guessed that she was here as her aunt's companion? she wondered, remembering Christine's warning about keeping her poverty a secret.

'That's rotten luck,' Kathleen said. 'But we're not going till eleven, you know. Surely she'll want to go to sleep before then?'

Muriel's eyes lit up; it was unlikely that her aunt would keep her much after eleven.

'I might be able to have half an hour – I'll try.'

'You'll not be dancing at all, though.' Andrew seemed to make no effort to hide his disappointment and a tingling of pleasure swept through her— No, she told herself, it was gratification she felt. She shook her head.

'I'm sorry.'

'What about this afternoon?' Bill interposed. 'How about exploring the ship and getting our bearings? Or perhaps you'd like some more deck games?' He smiled accommodatingly at them in turn. 'I'm willing to do anything— You choose, Muriel.'

'I'm willing to do anything *you* want,' she smiled. 'It's all new to me so I'll enjoy myself whatever we do.' She turned an anxious glance in Andrew's direction; it occurred to her that he might not want to be with her *all* the time. But there was a smile on his face and he suggested they meet after lunch and decide then what they would do.

Alone in her cabin, Muriel breathed a little sigh of contentment but, catching sight of herself in the mirror, a frown shaded her brow. 'He would never even have noticed me otherwise,' she reminded herself. 'It's the glamour that's attracted him; he likes it, so nothing else matters.' But it was an awful bother having to do all this every time she washed her face, she thought disconsolately, as she applied the glamour again before going out to join Mr. and Mrs. Worsley in the dining saloon.

Mrs. Worsley passed her the menu, telling her they had ordered sirloin steaks from the grill. Muriel ordered the same, finishing off with cherry pie and whipped cream. How her mother would love all this luxury, she thought, looking round the room with its mirrors and flowers and lovely maple panelling.

Her companions chatted the whole time, telling her they had met several more people they knew. They had seen Muriel and her friends on the sports deck, 'thoroughly enjoying themselves, by the look of things', and wasn't Muriel glad that they'd insisted on introducing her to such nice young men as Mr. Burke and Mr. Raines?

Muriel said yes, thanked them for doing so, and answered their questions about Aunt Edith.

'She thinks she'll be here for dinner tomorrow evening. She looked very ill this morning, but says she's sure to be better at the end of two days.'

Andrew came over then and, sitting in Aunt Edith's chair, talked sport for a few minutes with Mr. Worsley. Then he asked Muriel if she was ready. She couldn't decide whether or not it was imagination, but there seemed to be a hint of the proprietorial in his tone as he said,

'Yes? Well, then, let's be off.'

Certainly there was possessiveness in the way he took her arm, and Muriel felt herself quivering with an emotion that was both new and disturbing.

The afternoon flew on golden wings; Muriel had never been so blissfully happy in her life. She told herself it was because everything was so strange and exciting; because she was with pleasant people, and, for the first time since she could remember, she was away completely from jarring quarrels and oppressive disunion.

They followed Bill's suggestion and explored the ship, spent a lazy hour on deck, taking dips in the pool or merely lying in the sun, acquiring a tan. They took tea on the verandah, then attended the sports meeting in the lounge. A sports committee was formed with Mr. Worsley being elected as chairman.

'We'll see you about eleven, then?' Kathleen said when they came out.

'I'll try to be there, but I won't promise.' Muriel again felt Andrew's eyes regarding her strangely.

At eleven o'clock she suggested that her aunt might wish to go to sleep, but the old lady shook her head.

'Think I don't know the pool's open till midnight?' she said. 'Well, I do, my girl, and you're staying here for another half hour at least. What's the matter with you? Have you finished your book?'

'I'm tired of reading.'

'Tired of sitting here with me, you mean. Say it, child, I don't mind!'

'I came as your companion,' Muriel returned quietly, 'so I must therefore make your wishes my first consideration.'

'What a martyr you sound.' The old eyes glinted with sudden humour, then darkened almost at once. 'I suppose you believe I'm enjoying your company?' and when Muriel remained silent, 'I'm not! For one thing, your face annoys me – do you wash all that stuff off or just plaster more on top?'

Still no reply. Muriel sat upright in the chair by the bed, her hands clasped tightly in her lap, looking exceedingly sorry for herself.

'What time is it?' asked her aunt after what seemed an eternity to Muriel.

'Ten past eleven.'

'Is that all?' Aunt Edith grunted impatiently and sat up to shake her pillow. 'You're a damned nuisance, Muriel; I wish I'd never brought you! You're more trouble than a baby!'

'If you don't want me why can't I go? I'll give you my promise that I'll go straight to my cabin.'

'And nip into a bathing suit and be off like a shot to the pool? No, my girl, you stay here where I can see you. I don't know what sort of tricks you'll be up to, parading on deck at midnight with practically nothing on!'

'We wouldn't be parading on the deck! And what tricks—?' She pulled herself up abruptly. To pursue such a subject might result in unspeakable embarrassment. No telling what Aunt Edith might come out with. But, strangely, it was the thought that her aunt distrusted Andrew which made her angry. He was good and fine and decent. She knew it, and Aunt Edith would know it, too, when she had met him. 'If I promise you I'll go straight to bed will you let me go?'

Her aunt hesitated; she was tired, and heartily sick of the girl. Who would have thought she'd have to be watched like this?

'You promise?'

'Yes, Aunt Edith.'

'Very well, be off with you, then ... and Muriel ...'

'Yes?'

'I shall ask you in the morning if you've kept that promise. And don't think you can lie to me, because I'm very shrewd.'

'I have no intention of breaking my promise,' Muriel said stiffly, and left the cabin.

At six o'clock the following evening Aunt Edith sought Muriel out on deck. The introductions over, she and Andrew surveyed each other with unveiled astonishment.

His height alone would attract attention anywhere, thought Aunt Edith, tilting her head right back to examine with approval the finely-moulded features, the firm cast of his mouth, the broad line of his shoulders. She felt at a complete loss to account for his interest in Muriel; now if the child had been her natural, demure little self....

Andrew's surprise was even greater than hers. In startling contrast to her niece's clothes, there was no pretention to fashion in the black silk dress which hung rather untidily on her small, bony figure; her hair was grey and wispy and so thin that her scalp shone pinkly through it. Her chin was pointed and aggressive, her eyes, set in a tiny wrinkled face, were regarding her niece with marked disapproval. He frowned. If the old lady disapproved of the girl why had she brought her? –

for it was clear that Muriel had to do as she was told, therefore her aunt must have paid for the trip.

He dismissed the matter with a shrug of his shoulders and turned to say something to Bill. Muriel heaved a sigh of relief, for it was plain that her aunt was favourably impressed by Andrew. Then a little shadow crossed her face as she wondered how much free time her aunt would allow her. But she *had* promised her some, and she had announced her intention of keeping to her habit of going to bed at ten o'clock.

Aunt Edith was very good company and soon she had the whole party laughing at one of her jokes. She had married a bluff Lancashire cotton magnate, enormously wealthy but, Andrew soon gathered, a raw product. From him she had acquired both her forthrightness and her accent. Her amazing wit was undoubtedly a gift and she was soon to become, as always, the most popular person on board.

She lived in a small cottage at the end of a row of four which she owned; she did all her own housework and gardening and openly admitted that she managed on her rents. She also admitted quite frankly that she would walk miles for her eggs if she heard of one farmer selling them a penny a dozen cheaper than the rest. Yes, concluded Andrew, a truly remarkable woman was Aunt Edith; a skinflint, undoubtedly, but he liked her.

At the dinner table her wit flowed; Mr. Worsley had a loud and infectious laugh and the people at the adjacent table, unable to resist it, joined in, looking slightly envious and most likely wishing they could move a little nearer to the woman who was causing all this hilarity.

When dinner was over Mr. Worsley, reluctant to let her go, pressed her to join him and his wife at tombola in the lounge.

'I want to hear some more,' he chuckled, wiping his eyes. 'I don't know how you remember them all. The only ones I seem able to remember are – well, not exactly the drawing-room type.'

'Yes?' Aunt Edith's face was wooden. 'But those are not really funny, are they? As for my store, I've been on about thirty cruises and I suppose I've heard hundreds, so that whatever the conversation one or two come to mind.'

She agreed to join them, and remained with them for the rest of the trip, leaving Muriel quite free to do what she liked.

'I needn't have brought you, after all,' she told her, thinking of the money she could have saved. 'But one can't always be sure of joining up with nice people like the Worsleys. However, now that you are here, enjoy yourself. I like that Mr. Burke and I don't think you'll come to any harm with him – not that I can see what he finds attractive in a hussy like you, I'm sure,' she added with a glance of distaste at Muriel's very brief shorts.

Muriel coloured and said nothing. For some reason she had begun to wish she could start all over again. Her own clothes, she knew, were totally unsuitable for a trip like this, yet she would have given anything to have them here. Her little white dance dress, her own swimsuit, and her one best afternoon dress with its lace collar which fastened primly up to her neck. Upon reflection, however, she realized that, even if she had them here, she couldn't wear them now without causing some considerable astonishment. Besides, she thought dejectedly, without her glamour she wouldn't have received a second glance from Andrew.

She found him a charming companion and, she

mused happily, he must like her, too, for he spent every available moment with her. They swam together, played deck games, and took part in all the sports and competitions arranged by the entertainments committee. They danced together every evening and strolled on deck afterwards, and the only spot of imperfection was that she had to be continually on her guard; had to maintain the whole time her air of worldly sophistication.

On the third evening they came on deck, alone for the first time, and they walked its length in silence, a pleasant companionable silence without trace of awkwardness or strain.

They stopped and leant against the rail. A still and silent night with a canopy of stars above and a tranquil sea glistening like a frost-coated field on a moonlit winter's eve. Muriel found herself in a state of magic unreality. Andrew's nearness set her heart racing and it seemed quite natural that he should kiss her. He whispered things, too, as his lips caressed her hair; subtle, exciting things about their future. The wild fluttering of her heart she took to be triumph, exultation at her amazing victory. Rich beyond her wildest expectations ... and he had fallen in love with her!

And so, when she left him, she wrote and told her cousin of her 'great piece of luck'. 'I never thought it could be so simple,' she continued, driven on by elation, 'and I must admit that at first I did not intend trying my luck on him because I didn't like him very much. However, when I saw he was attracted to me I thought it would be foolish to waste the opportunity, for he's very rich indeed.' About to add his name, she hesitated. No, she must be present to witness Christine's astonishment on hearing who he was. Wouldn't she be amazed? Perhaps she even knew him. She must know the firm, because the tall tower with its glittering neon sign was a landmark in Barston.

The following morning the ship anchored off Funchal, and after that day in Madeira Muriel knew that her feelings towards Andrew were very different from what she had supposed.

The four of them met at the gangway on 'D' deck as arranged, and boarded the launch together. The hawkers promptly brought their boats alongside, holding up their wares and shouting the prices in broken English. Muriel was fascinated by them; she wanted to buy so much, but had so little money. However, she did buy an embroidered tablecloth each for her mother and Dil. For her mother she also bought three fancy shopping baskets which fitted one inside the other, and when one man held up a wicker bedroom chair she would have bought that, too, had not Andrew stopped her.

'The duty will be too much,' he warned. 'You can buy one cheaper at home.'

'But that's not the same; this one has "Madeira" worked across the back.'

'I wouldn't buy it,' he said with quiet authority. 'There are always rows of these things left in the customs sheds, you'll see them when we get back.'

Muriel prudently took his advice, and as this reminded her that duty would have to be paid on what she had already bought, she decided against any further purchases at present.

They took a motor trip, visiting the wine lodges where they sat in the courtyard and sampled the wine offered them by the wine dealer. They continued by the coast road to Santa Cruz, climbed to Santo da Serra, stopping there for lunch and then returning to Funchal by the mountain road. During the drive,

Muriel, entranced by the scenery, had the greatest difficulty in maintaining her role. The impulsive and childish habit of clapping her hands to give outlet to her excitement had many times to be sternly suppressed. In spite of this, however, she did make a few slips and, although the other two didn't appear to notice, Andrew's head would always turn sharply and his eyes subject her to a very searching scrutiny. If she wasn't very careful, she thought fearfully, she'd make a complete hash of things.

'I have such lots and lots to buy,' Kathleen exclaimed when they arrived at the shopping centre. She had plenty of money and when she ran short of escudo notes the shopkeepers were only too willing to accept English money. She bought lovely flimsy underwear, an embroidered bed-jacket and several pieces of imitation jewellery which Muriel thought rather gaudy.

At length Muriel asked Andrew how much duty she would have to pay on what she had bought from the boats.

'I should say about five pounds,' he replied, watching her curiously. 'Aren't you going to buy one of those pretty bed-jackets?'

Muriel shook her head, then, noticing his odd expression, she remarked airily,

'I have so many, though these are, of course, perfectly entrancing.' Christine always said things were 'perfectly entrancing' or 'just too heavenly'. 'I think I'll have one of these blouses, though.' And that was all she bought.

Kathleen was undecided about a handbag, and Muriel's face was a little wistful as she watched her holding it up.

'Shall I?' Kathleen asked Bill. 'What do you think of it?'

'I don't know much about these things,' he replied with a laugh, 'but I'll buy it for you if you want it.' He picked up another. 'I think I prefer this one. What do you think, Muriel?'

'I like it very much,' she said, fingering it. 'The other is too large – for me, that is. I like small handbags.' Unconsciously she had turned to Andrew, and he quickly dropped his eyelids to hide his expression of amused contempt. Then he offered to buy a bag for her. She looked startled, wondering if, somehow, she had given the impression that she wanted him to buy her a handbag.

'Oh, no! I didn't – I mean – if I wanted one I would buy it myself,' she stammered, and once again Andrew's brow creased in perplexity.

'You should never refuse the offer of a present,' he said. 'Which one would you like? How about this?' He held it up, apparently intrigued by the gilt and ivory clasp.

'Do you like it?' she asked shyly.

'Yes, very much.'

Muriel hesitated, but looking anxiously up at him she found him smiling.

'Then I'll have it,' she said, unaware of the child-like pleasure and gratitude in her eyes. 'Thank you very much.'

Andrew bit his lip in vexation; was he finding himself baffled by a woman at last? he wondered.

Bill was spending on the most ridiculous trifles, but Andrew, like Muriel, went for the lovely embroidery, buying several tablecloths and dozens of handkerchiefs – women's handkerchiefs, Muriel noticed with a little sinking feeling. He added to her uncertainty by picking up a pretty dress in white lace with brightly coloured sprays of flowers on the bodice and hem.

'Will this fit a girl of fourteen?' he asked her vaguely. 'A rather tall fourteen?'

'Yes, I think so.' A girl of fourteen . . . He was quite old enough to have a daughter of that age. . . .

Andrew, suddenly noticing her expression, said with faint mockery,

'It's for my sister,' and gave a satisfied smile at her obvious relief. He never made mistakes where women were concerned.

The shopping finished, Bill and Kathleen said they were going back to the ship, and after accompanying them to the launch and handing over their own parcels, Andrew and Muriel strolled along the waterfront. He found nothing new, but he obligingly walked and walked, answering her numerous questions with patience and sometimes with amusement. A flower girl in native costume came up to them, displaying her wares. Andrew chose mountain flowers in preference to those from the gardens, and after the girl had moved on he turned to pin them to Muriel's dress. It was cut very low and as his fingers lightly touched her flesh Muriel trembled as a feeling of sheer rapture swept over her, and her eyes were warm and glowing as they met his. There was a hushed and tense little moment as an entirely new and baffling expression entered Andrew's eyes. It seemed to Muriel that he was annoyed with himself for some reason. Then he said, with a strange, half-smothered little laugh,

'If you look at me like that I'll be tempted to kiss you right here,' and before she could think of anything to say he took her arm and they resumed their walk – this time much more briskly than before.

CHAPTER THREE

THEY dined at a small hotel, not making their way back to the quay until the lights had sprung up all around them. Reaching the ship, they did not join the others, but stayed on deck until midnight.

'Well, have you enjoyed yourself?' Andrew asked, slipping an arm round her waist.

'It was wonderful!' She looked up, giving him a rapturous smile. 'Thank you for taking me, Andrew. I should have been so lonely if I hadn't met you – and yet I was dreadfully embarrassed when Mrs. Worsley offered to introduce us.'

'Were you, Muriel?'

'Yes, but I'm glad she insisted.'

'So am I,' he said truthfully. 'But I can't agree about your being lonely if we hadn't met. You underrate yourself, my dear; a girl like you will never be lacking in admirers.'

She didn't like his tone, and her eyes sought his again; but he was smiling in a way that thrilled her and she dismissed the idea that he had spoken mockingly. That little inflection was just a permanent part of his make-up.

When she made no comment Andrew bent and kissed her hard on the mouth. Muriel was strangely disturbed by that kiss; she felt a sudden rush of blood to her cheeks, but his arms about her were gentle and she returned his kiss in total ignorance of his inner contempt and amusement.

And in that moment she knew she loved him; that, whatever came of this, she would never again be the same girl who had served in her father's shop only five days ago.

Her sudden realization brought with it a tremor of fear. Supposing she were wrong in thinking he loved her . . . ?

Andrew felt her tremble and drew her more closely into his arms.

'Are you cold, dear?'

'No.' She uttered a shaky laugh of relief. How warm and safe she felt against him . . . and how stupid were her fears. Andrew wouldn't hold her like this unless he loved her. 'Just – perfectly happy,' she whispered in a voice husky with emotion. 'Are you happy, too?'

'I think I'm always happy,' he answered, and there was a little silence before Muriel said, her eyes clouding unconsciously,

'How wonderful to be able to say that.'

'Why, aren't you always happy?'

'Not always.' She hastily changed the subject, lest he should ask about her home life. 'I didn't buy those stamps for Derek. I do wish I hadn't forgotten, he reminded me so many times to collect all the stamps I could from every place we visited. He's a very enthusiastic philatelist since he went to the grammar school,' she explained.

'You can get them at the bureau on "B" deck,' he told her. 'In any case, I have some; you can take those,' and after a pause, 'Derek is your brother?'

'Yes; he's just twelve.' She thanked him for the stamps and after another pause he asked her about her family. She told him a little – a very little – and then again changed the subject. Andrew's eyes became veiled and perceptive; he didn't press her further, but turned her face up and kissed her.

'Good night, Muriel,' he said gently. 'I'll see you at

the pool in the morning.'

'Good night, Andrew, and thank you again for giving me such a lovely day.'

Entering her cabin, the first thing she noticed was the letter she had written to Christine; her heart missed a beat as relief poured through her. Thank goodness she had forgotten to post it; her cousin must never think she had married Andrew for anything but love. On a sudden happy impulse she sat down and, tired as she was, wrote another letter to her cousin.

When she was in bed she thought, drowsily, but with a chuckle, when Christine reads that she'll think I'm crazy! Well, she was a little crazy, she supposed – and hoped she would remain in that state for the rest of her life.

The following morning her aunt came into her cabin just as she was putting the finishing touches to her hair. The old lady eyed her distastefully but made no comment on her appearance.

'Aren't you ready yet?' she asked, glancing at her watch.

'I won't be a minute, Aunt Edith.' Muriel hunted in the drawer for a handkerchief and when she turned her aunt was standing by the desk.

'*Two* letters for Christine? I thought I told you not to have anything to do with that girl!'

'Oh—' Picking up the letter on the pad, Muriel put it into her bag. 'That one isn't important now,' she said, and, tearing it across, tossed it into the waste paper basket. 'Just one more moment, Aunt Edith, I've forgotten my perfume.'

'Perfume . . .!' The old lady turned away in resignation and disgust; but as Muriel went into the bathroom she bent down and retrieved the letter.

'Well!' She could hardly believe her eyes. 'Well—'

'How dare you!' Snatching at the letter, her niece tore it into little scraps. 'You have no right to read my letters!' Muriel blushed with shame as she dropped the pieces in the basket again.

'How dare I?' Aunt Edith looked at her scathingly. 'You ought to be ashamed of yourself! I've never read anything so – so uncontrolled in my life. To think that you, a sensible girl, could write such drivel! Are you out of your mind?'

'I didn't send it, did I?' Muriel burst out defensively, thinking that 'drivel' was certainly not the word she would have expected her aunt to use. 'I've written another – quite different this time.'

'I should hope so!' Then she added impatiently, 'Come on, child, we're late already!'

Three days later there was another call, this time at Casablanca. Kathleen and Bill, both having visited the Sultan's palace at Rabat, preferred to spend the afternoon at the seaside resort of Fedala, so Andrew and Muriel went to Rabat alone, in the car Andrew had hired privately. Once again everything she saw delighted Muriel. The Sultan's palace and gardens threw her into ecstasies, but Muriel was careful to suppress her impulsiveness, keeping her remarks light and casual and accompanying them sometimes with the hint of a yawn.

Andrew watched her with a mixture of puzzlement and humour. It really was amusing, he thought, the way those eyes would become very big and round and serious when they were meant to allure him; at other times they would be coquettishly veiled under thickly curling lashes, or flickering with a faintly bored expression. But there were times when they would be very candid and innocent, and it was then that Andrew would be pricked by vague and uneasy doubts. He wished only to see her as an easy, grasping woman of the world, but he often glimpsed a child, a rather enchanting child of delicate instincts and timid reserve. He was used to women, he knew their ways, he told himself angrily, and this was just part of the act; it was no novelty, he'd seen it scores of times before; the worldly woman adopting an air of innocence. And yet he wished Muriel wouldn't do it. When she was her natural self he knew where he stood, he felt safe, he enjoyed himself, and looked forward to the time when she would discover that he had been playing with her, that she had been wasting time which, to her, must be very precious. But when she adopted that air of childish innocence it worried him, it brought on these doubts and gave him a queer little feeling inside when he thought of the final parting between them.

They had walked to Sale, home of the Corsairs of the sixteenth century; they had explored the native quarter, then picked up the car again and gone on to the Oudaia Gardens, where they were having tea.

He found his eyes drawn irresistibly to Muriel as she leant back in her chair, gazing dreamily about her, her lips parted temptingly, the sunbeams glinting through her hair, seeming to set it on fire.... He'd never seen such hair! What did it look like when it was down? – falling on to her shoulders—? Andrew pulled himself up, scowling at his thoughts. What the devil did he care, anyway? This was a pleasant summer pastime; in a week it would be over, in a month, almost forgotten – and Muriel with it.

She had turned, meeting his gaze placidly; he looked rather mockingly amused, but she didn't mind that at all, because, in her inexperience, she read complete sincerity in his expression, too. She sighed blissfully and told him she would never, never forget this holiday. Andrew's smile deepened; he wondered what she would say if he told her of his thoughts of only a moment ago. But, as they continued to look into each other's eyes, he began to have the odd little conviction that he would not forget Muriel so easily. It was as though time stood still for a brief spell, giving him the chance to look carefully, to think, to learn ... before he did something he would regret. Regret? Andrew frowned heavily as the word flashed through his brain. What strange ideas came into his head these days. He was most unlikely to do anything he'd regret. As he turned his head a little sigh escaped Muriel. What had caused that sudden frown? she wondered, her eyes still fixed on his face. To her there had been something magical in that moment as their eyes held each other's, and if Andrew had turned again he would have surprised an expression that revealed the secret of her heart far more eloquently than any words could have done. But he didn't turn, and when they were in the car again he kept his eyes on the scenery, looking steadily out of the window and not even speaking to her.

Back on the ship, he took both their keys from the steward on duty and, giving Muriel hers, bade her a brief and rather curt good night.

Muriel felt that chill fingers had been spread over her heart. She had vexed him somehow, and she couldn't bring herself to ask about it. How easily he could hurt her, she realized, and wondered if it would always be so. If only he didn't look quite so austere, so formidable, she could have taken his hand, given it a little squeeze, and asked him what she had done wrong. She could have reached up and put her arms round his neck and told him how much he was hurting her, and that a smile would reassure her, a kiss make her whole world rosy again. Yes, that was how it ought to be ... but would she and Andrew ever be quite so intimate as that?

A troubled sigh escaped her; she quivered, 'Good night, Andrew,' and walked dejectedly away towards the stairs. He hadn't said a word about meeting her at the pool in the morning. She thought with sudden panic that perhaps he didn't love her, after all; perhaps he didn't want her any more—

'Muriel!' Her name seemed to escape against his will; she turned as he strode towards her, and he noticed the tears in her eyes as she lifted her face to his.

'Andrew....' she whispered convulsively, and then she was in his arms, her head against his breast, her hand clutching the lapel of his coat as though she would never let him go. 'Were you – were you vexed with me?' Sophisticated women preserved their decorum in any situation, she thought, aware that a tear had fallen on to the front of Andrew's shirt, but she didn't want to be sophisticated any more; she just wanted to be natural, to be loved until her immaculate hair became tumbled and her dress disarranged. She raised her head and saw through the mist blurring her vision that Andrew's dark eyes held a quality of remorse.

'Muriel, my little love....' The moonlight cast into high relief the beauty and the delicacy of her face. Andrew bent to kiss her quivering lips, with infinite tenderness at first, but as the trembling of her body fanned his desire to a flame his mouth was as ruthless as the arms that held her. 'I want you,' he whispered hoarsely. 'You're a witch, Muriel, an enchantress.'

Slowly sanity returned; his lips were gentle again as they caressed her hair.

'Did I hurt you, sweetheart?'

'Terribly.' But her eyes were radiant and laughing as they look up into his. 'I loved it, though.'

Andrew laughed softly, kissed her again and then, with mock severity, he told her it was high time she thought of sleep.

'I could stay here all night,' she said, but trotted meekly beside him as he took her hand and made for the stairs. Outside her cabin they paused and Muriel asked again if he were vexed about something.

'No, my dearest, I wasn't.' He smiled, so tenderly, and after touching her forehead with his lips he said softly, 'Good night, darling, and sleep well. I'll see you at the pool in the morning.'

The final port of call was Lisbon. After a sightseeing tour in the afternoon, they returned to the ship for dinner and then left again for the casino at Estoril. Bill and Kathleen were attracted to the gaming tables, but Andrew, to Muriel's profound relief, said he preferred to dance.

He was very quiet for most of the time, and Muriel was quite content with her own happy thoughts. The future was just one long and blissful walk through Paradise, with new delights on which she would not allow her mind to dwell. It struck her that Andrew had talked very little about his home, but then there had been so many other things to talk about. And, apart from those wonderful moments on deck after the dancing had finished at midnight, they had not had much time alone together.

Andrew had no father; he lived with his mother and sister in a Georgian mansion set high on a hill overlooking a large forest. His mother bred dogs and goats, very special goats which won prizes at all the shows.

That was all she knew about Andrew's family, though he had once mentioned a married sister.

'A penny for them.' Muriel leant away from him and looked up. Not one word had he spoken to her all through the dance. 'You look so serious.'

'Yes?' Andrew led her off the floor as the music stopped. 'Do you want something to drink?' he asked as they sat down. Muriel shook her head.

'Don't you want to sell them?' she said teasingly.

'I wasn't thinking of anything important, Muriel.' He was more than a little bored, and wondered why. He certainly wasn't bored with Muriel; at the thought a rueful light entered his eyes. Where was he heading? What was this strange magnetism she possessed for him? – this all-compelling charm he had found lacking in every woman he had ever met? He was treading on dangerous ground; he thought of something Bill had jokingly said about being careful not to get 'caught'.

Well, he would never be caught by a woman of this type. Thank goodness there were only two more days .... His thoughts drifted in circles, he always found himself back to the question, 'Where was he heading?'

It was two o'clock in the morning before they returned to the ship; Andrew was still quiet and thoughtful and a dumb little ache began to tug at Muriel's heart when, reaching her cabin, he took hold of her hand and raised it to his lips.

'What is it, my dear?' he said gently.

'Nothing. Nothing's the matter now.' How easily he sensed her little fears and worries; how very close they were, how perfectly suited to each other mentally as well as physically. Her heart swelled with love for him and with an impetuous movement she put her arms round his neck and, standing on her toes, stretched up to kiss him on the lips; for an astonished moment he did not respond, then his arms went round her and his mouth pressed hard on hers.

'I really must let you go,' he said, ten minutes later. 'What would your aunt say if she knew you were out here with me at this time of the morning?'

'She'd be terribly shocked, I'm afraid. Good night, dearest Andrew – oh, yes, I know, but good night sounds so much more romantic.'

'Then good night,' he said softly, and turned away to his own cabin where he lay awake for the rest of the night.

Only two more days. Muriel, in spite of the knowledge that the future held far more happiness than she had ever known, sighed for the lovely days that had gone. She had been with Andrew the whole time, a time of dreamlike unreality in which her love, allowed to take its own ecstatic course, had so completely overshadowed her original design as to render it almost imaginary. Not that the thoughts of it didn't produce a blush of shame whenever she recalled it, but it seemed so vague and unimportant that she very seldom did recall it.

There had been times when Andrew had hurt her by some cynical glance or sarcastic remark, but it was all forgotten when he made love to her at night. There had also been many times when, forgetful of all but her own love for him, glimpses of her real self had peeped out. Andrew had frowned, then, and she had immediately reverted to her worldly manner.

Muriel heaved a little sigh of regret as she got into bed. If only Andrew had been different from other men; if only he hadn't wanted glamour. But it was very plain that he did want it. Poise and elegance, glamour and sophistication; he never frowned at those, they were what he required in his wife, therefore he should have them. She would do anything, she told herself with firm resolve, *anything* to keep his love and make him happy.

On the last evening there was a special dance, but Andrew, who had been oddly restless and irritable all day, suggested they go on deck. Everything was calm and they stood by the rail in silence, Andrew's arm about her waist, his head bent to touch hers. This was sheer heaven, she thought rapturously as her lips met his in eager response. Andrew had brought her here to discuss their future, to arrange their next meeting. How lucky that they lived within reasonable distance of each other ... and she suddenly felt very sorry for Bill and Kathleen whom she had seen exchanging addresses.

'Still happy, Muriel?' he asked, his cool breath stirring her hair.

'You know I am – because it's all due to you.' She laughed softly and leant away from him, looking at him with a sort of humble gratitude in her lovely eyes. 'I haven't told you yet that I love you – I've been thinking there must be lots and lots of eloquent ways of saying it, but I can't think of one.' She was not in the least embarrassed; her colour did not rise or her voice falter as she went on, simply, 'I love you, Andrew. I shall love you for ever.' He had never used the word love, but she attached no importance to that omission. Between them, words did not matter, she thought, snuggling contentedly against him. She just *knew* that he loved her.

Andrew gave a strange little laugh and kissed her upturned face. But there was an almost brutal roughness in that kiss, it lacked respect, and Muriel recoiled from him, as stupefied as if he had insulted her. Her big eyes stared at him in bewilderment, and her lips trembled in sudden fear and doubt.

'Andrew, I didn't like that,' she whispered, half in apology, half in reproach.

Andrew's lip curled slightly; he had to hand it to her, she was clever – but not quite clever enough to realize that neither her wits nor her play-acting were a match for his.

'I'm sorry; I thought you liked my kisses.'

She looked up at him like an unhappy child, imploring him to say something that would sweep away her terrible fear and bewilderment. He remained silent, his eyes expressionless, but an unmistakable touch of mockery about his lips.

'You – you've kissed me like that once before,' she said tremulously, 'and I didn't like it then.'

Another silence followed before Andrew took her gently to him and kissed her again.

'Is that better?' His eyes were alight with amusement and she could find no words with which to answer him. For the first time since they had met the silence between them became oppressive. Andrew stirred impatiently and suggested a stroll. Mutely she walked beside him.

'Perhaps we'd better go and dance, after all,' he said irritably at last.

'Very well.'

At midnight they came on deck again; Andrew seemed a million miles away – yet he held her hand. He led her to the rail and as she cast him a hesitant sideways glance she noticed the little white lines at the corners of his mouth, the strange tension of his lips, compressed as though in stern self-mastery.

'This is goodbye, Muriel,' he said lightly. 'Shall we make it as brief as possible?'

'Goodbye. . . .' She had known it all the evening –

that kiss had told her plainly that he felt neither love nor respect for her – and yet she stared at him unbelievingly. 'You don't mean that,' she cried in anguish and desperation. 'You don't, Andrew – please say you're – you're only joking! You can't mean that you never want to see me again.' Her tone had dropped to a pleading whisper, bringing a quick frown to his brow and the return of all his doubts and uneasiness. But after a moment he shrugged his shoulders lightly.

'These shipboard flirtations are most enjoyable while they last, my dear, but they're not to be taken seriously; you must have known that?'

'Flirtation?' All her worldly poise had left her and a terrible sob choked the words. 'Is that all it meant to you?' This wasn't really happening, she thought wildly, Andrew couldn't want this to be the end. They were meant for each other, surely he could see that. She opened her mouth to tell him, but the words died on her lips. What to her had been a sweet and lovely thing had been to him ... a mere flirtation. Yes, this was the end; Andrew never wanted to see her again.

'Don't let's spoil everything by stupid pretence.' His words broke pitilessly into her thoughts. 'We've both enjoyed ourselves; let's call it a day and part friends.'

Muriel bent her head as though she had been struck; her hands dropped to her sides as every emotion left her. Through the obscure mist of her brain only one fact emerged: Andrew was nothing more than a heartless flirt, a man who amused himself by making love to unsuspecting women and then trampling on their love with callous indifference. He really wasn't worth a second thought....

Unconsciously she clasped her hands and held them tightly against her breast, against the dull throbbing pain that was in her heart, and as she looked up she saw that Andrew's eyes were fixed upon them with a strange and brooding expression. But then his smile appeared, flippant and mocking, sending a spasm of pain through her whole body. Her lovely eyes drooped again, but after a little while she regained command of herself and was able to say, with a calmness that amazed her,

'Yes, you're right; we have both enjoyed ourselves,' and she managed to laugh, too, a flippant laugh which matched his own mood to perfection. 'You said we'd make our parting brief, so I'll just say – goodbye.' And without giving him time to utter another word she was gone.

Andrew stood quite still, watching her until she had passed out of sight, then, turning, he leant against the rail, conscious of a state of restlessness upon which he did not want to dwell, and a sense of guilt he could not understand.

One glance had told him what she was; he'd only given her a well-deserved lesson. Why, then, this feeling of guilt? What had happened to the triumph, the amusement he was to have derived from this final parting? His triumph appeared to have become inexpressibly bitter, his amusement replaced by the dreary conviction that Muriel's stricken face would haunt him for the rest of his days.

She had stood beside him so quietly, her great eyes brimming with suppressed tears, her hands clasped tightly together as though in unconscious prayer. Her poise and her worldliness had been stripped from her, she had seemed like a child, defenceless and unspeakably hurt.

What nonsense! Andrew shook himself impatiently. She was a woman, a woman who had been playing for high stakes – and lost. That was the only reason for that stricken look, for the fact that she was almost in tears.

At last he turned away; he was glad the cruise was over. It would be a long while before he was persuaded to take another. Bill could find someone else next year, unless. ... A faint smile touched his lips; Bill seemed to be the one in danger of being caught. But she was a nice girl, Kathleen, he liked her very much.

The ship docked at nine o'clock the next morning; As Bill had taken the earlier breakfast with Kathleen, Andrew had his alone. Muriel, he noticed, was absent, and when he had finished he went over to say goodbye to her aunt and the Worsleys.

'Goodbye, Mr. Burke.' Aunt Edith's face was devoid of expression. 'Perhaps we shall meet again some time.'

'Perhaps.' Andrew smiled courteously. 'Is Muriel unwell?'

'She has a headache.'

'I'm – sorry.' He met her level gaze for a moment, then his brows lifted in a gesture of arrogance. 'I hope she'll soon be better,' he said, and turned to Mr. Worsley.

'I wonder ...' said Aunt Edith to herself some time later as she caught sight of Andrew and Bill as they disembarked. 'I wonder if he knew what the little minx was up to? He struck me from the first as a man with exceptional powers of observation.'

CHAPTER FOUR

THE heart attack was as severe as it was sudden; it occurred one morning as Mr. Paterson was shaving in the bathroom, and only then did his family learn that he had been visiting the doctor for over twelve months.

Mrs. Paterson was superb in her role of grief-stricken widow; Dil's only emotion was one of resentment that her father had left so little. To Muriel, it seemed that only Derek shared her deep sorrow – and even he, at times, was able to laugh as though nothing had happened.

One day, late in October, Muriel, after trudging for miles in the mist and drizzle, arrived home tired and dispirited to find her mother out and her sister reading by the fire. There was no sign of a meal and an unfamiliar sharpness edged Muriel's voice as she said,

'Dil, I think you could at least have the tea ready.'

'Oh, do you?' snapped her sister. 'You seem to forget I'm ill. You wouldn't care a rap if I strained myself!'

'There's not much fear of that,' Muriel retorted. 'And as for being ill, having a baby's the most natural thing in the world.'

'Is it? You wait till you're having one yourself, then you'll not talk like that!'

Muriel winced and turned away.

'I think you coddle yourself too much,' she said, searching in the drawer for a tablecloth. 'It doesn't do you any good to be idle all day—'

'Shut up! When you begin working yourself you can pass an opinion. But please don't do so while my husband is helping to keep you!'

Muriel spun round, the angry colour fusing her face.

'He is not! Mother is spending the money we had for the shop. How dare you say such a thing!'

'Proud, eh?' Dil said hatefully. 'You're right about Mother, she is spending the shop money, and more rapidly than you think. But not on housekeeping – on clothes, on rubbish. Whether you like it or not our contribution to this house is helping to keep you, and the sooner you face the fact the better. You're not looking for work.'

'Are you suggesting I'm walking the streets of Barston for amusement?' Muriel demanded hotly.

'If you really wanted work you'd take the job Fred's pal offered you!'

Muriel hesitated, then went into the kitchen to prepare the tea. Dil was right, she ought to accept the job; the money was good, and sorely needed. 'But I'd rather starve than go and work there,' she told herself fiercely. 'He'd be sure to think I was running after him.'

Her family knew nothing of what happened on the cruise; they just thought her plan had failed. Disgusted, they had told her she hadn't gone the right way about it, then the matter had been dropped. Only to Christine had Muriel told the truth, naturally keeping Andrew's name a secret. Christine, also disgusted at her failure, had said that falling in love herself was the very thing she should have guarded against. Muriel had not seen her cousin since, nor had she seen Aunt Edith, and the cruise and its lost chances were forgotten by everyone except Muriel. Never, for one conscious moment, was Andrew completely out of her thoughts. Even when, a month after her return, her father died, the memory of Andrew was with her all the time, adding to her unhappiness.

When the shop was sold Muriel had looked for work without success; then Fred had come home with the news that a pal of his could find her a job in the factory where he worked. His offer had seemed heaven-sent, until Fred mentioned the name of the firm. Muriel had instantly rejected it and her mother and sister, angry and astonished, had told her outright that she could not expect them to keep her; she must earn her own living, and without further delay. Muriel had held out, but her sister had never allowed the matter to drop and she mentioned it again at tea time.

'I do think you should take it before it's too late,' Mrs. Paterson added. 'Dil's right, you know, Muriel, you can't go on like this indefinitely.'

'Her trouble is that she's too particular,' Dil snapped. 'The job's not good enough for her.'

'It isn't that; you know I would be willing to take any sort of job—'

'Then why don't you? – oh, she makes me sick! Mother, you should force her to take it!'

'What is it, Muriel?' Fred's voice was quieter than his wife's, but just as impatient. 'You must have realized by this time that you can't afford to be too particular.'

'And we can't afford to keep her any longer,' Dil added.

'Dil's right; the shop money won't last more than another few weeks,' her mother warned, and Muriel's eyes strayed to the new dress flung carelessly over the back of a chair. Her mother had gone out, she recollected, to buy Derek a school blazer and cap.

'Why can't you leave Muriel alone?' Derek, his 'Approach to Latin' beside his plate, looked up and winked at her. 'You stick it out, old girl; let them nag their bally heads off – but don't be pushed into a scruffy job like that.'

'Be quiet!' Dil glared at him. 'And get on with your tea – or your homework, whichever you're supposed to be doing.'

'Oh, you!' he retorted rudely. 'You'd make anyone sick with your temper. I wish to goodness this pesky baby would come, then perhaps we'd get some peace – though I suppose it'll scrike like the very dickens,' he added, half under his breath.

'Derek!' His mother rapped him smartly over the knuckles with her knife. 'You forget yourself! – and how many times have I told you to keep the slang you learn from comics out of your conversation? When you've finished your tea you can go to bed.'

'Don't I always go to my room when I've had my tea?' he flashed back. 'Couldn't do my homework down here if I wanted to, with all this nagging going on. Muriel, will you come up later and tell me if my algebra's right?'

'Yes, I'll come.' What a life for Derek, she thought miserably, having to go to his room in order to get away from the continual bickering.

'What a happy family we are,' she sighed, almost to herself. 'Why is it we're so different from other people?'

'We'd be happier if you were bringing in some money,' Dil sneered.

'Please be quiet,' Fred ordered impatiently. 'Muriel, what have you against this job? I admit it's not quite what you would have liked, but you can at least give it a trial. You can't keep on like this, even having to borrow your bus fares into Barston. Do be sensible, for heaven's sake!'

Muriel sat there picking at her food. It was quite natural for them to think she was being too particular, but how could she make them understand without telling them about Andrew? And that was unthinkable; their anger she could bear, but not their laughter and contempt.

Fred was talking again, and Dil, and her mother; they went on and on until Muriel could have fled from them all, not just up to her room, but miles and miles away, out of their lives for ever. But the idea was gone almost immediately; she would very soon come back, she thought. It was strange how you went on loving people no matter what they did to you. Her family loved her too, she felt sure of it. But they were angry with her, and who could blame them? Wasn't she being infuriatingly obstinate?

At last she looked up.

'In a large factory like that, do the – bosses ever see the ordinary workers? I mean, do they ever go into the departments? Mr. – Mr. – Groves, for instance?' No wonder they were all looking at her with unbounded astonishment, she thought, her cheeks colouring.

'What on earth has that to do with it?' Dil gasped.

'Nothing, really.'

'The "Groves" part of it doesn't exist now.' Fred eyed his sister-in-law with a very curious expression. 'Do you happen to know any of the bosses, Muriel?'

'How could she?' Mrs. Paterson interposed. 'Muriel never goes out.'

'Do you, Muriel?' Dil said evenly, ignoring her mother's remark. 'Do you know any of the bosses at Burke's?'

'No . . .' Her voice was scarcely audible. How could I?'

'In that case,' she said quietly, 'you'd better explain.'

'Explain?' Muriel's colour rose still higher; she shrugged her shoulders helplessly. 'I don't know what made me say it.' She looked at Fred. 'Peter did say he'd start me without experience, didn't he? – you told him that I've only helped Daddy in the shop?'

'Yes; he knows that. All the girls have to learn, it seems, and Peter will help you at first. Are you going to give it a trial?'

'You haven't explained, Muriel – don't change the subject.' For the moment Dil was no longer interested in the job; there was some mystery here, and she wanted to get to the bottom of it. But she had reckoned without her husband. Fred liked to mind his own business; if people wanted to be secretive about their affairs then it had nothing to do with anyone but themselves.

'You can let that drop now, Dil,' he said quietly. 'We're talking about something else.'

'But—'

'I said you can let it drop! Muriel, are you going to try this job?'

For another moment she hesitated, then she said in a flat little voice,

'Very well, Fred, I'll try it.'

And so, the following Monday morning, she started out at seven-thirty and was one of the thousands of men and women who trooped through the factory gates an hour later.

Her job was assembling parts for electric motors; Peter, who was the chargehand of the department, willingly assisted her and she very soon learnt the work. But she was far from happy; the vulgar jokes and conversation of the other girls sickened her, and although she worked conscientiously she lived for the sound of the buzzer. It soon became apparent to her workmates that she wasn't interested in their jokes, or their newest boy-friends, and after a few weeks she was left severely alone except for an odd occasion when she would hear some sarcastic remark about people who were 'stuck-up'.

She had been at the factory five weeks when Peter ordered the place to be 'cleaned up a bit'. Mr. Burke was on one of his routine inspections of the factory.

Muriel saw him enter, stop and speak to the foreman for a few minutes, nod to Peter, and then move on to where the girls were working. Every now and then he would stop to inquire about something; Muriel, her breath almost choking her, kept her head averted and prayed he would pass on without seeing her.

He was speaking to the girl next to her. The deep, familiar voice came to her quite clearly; Milly's respectful 'no, sir', and 'yes, sir', reached her as though from a long distance.

And then he was standing right in front of her; she knew instinctively that he had been about to pass on and then halted abruptly. He had recognized her, and at last she looked up, the hot colour flooding her cheeks as she became aware of the amused glances of the girls nearest to her. She was miserably aware, too, of her soiled overall, and of the difference Andrew must see in her.

His face was impassive, not a trace of recognition was betrayed in his coldly impersonal gaze.

'You're new, aren't you?' he asked, in the same curt tones he had used to the others. 'How long have you been here?'

'Five weeks,' she replied, almost in a whisper.

'Have you done this sort of work before?'

'No.' The situation seemed unreal, fantastic. She had often visualized a meeting between them, even while praying it would never take place, but she had never pictured anything like this. Not a trace of surprise, not a sign of recognition. She felt he must actually hate her.

'Are you – happy here?'

'Yes, thank you.' Surely, she thought, her eyes widening as she noticed the haughty lift of his brows, he didn't expect her to follow the other girls' example and call him sir!

'Are you on your own time yet?'

'I'm not quick enough to go on piecework,' she told him quietly, and for a brief moment they stared at each other in silence. It seemed strange that, with her heart beating to suffocation, her memory could take her back to the peace, the tranquillity, the perfect bliss of those days and nights on the ship. Then suddenly the only thing she recalled was her own impulsive confession of love, and Andrew's ruthless reaction to it; a shadow of pain crossed her face and, unconsciously, a look of reproach entered her eyes. But Andrew regarded her change of expression with indifference and after making a few remarks to the foreman, who was standing beside him, he turned and left the room. And then his calm deserted him; he strode across the yard towards the offices, his hands clenched, his face pale with anger. To see her again, just when he had begun to forget! For three months she had continually intruded into his thoughts, and now, when he was finding it less and less difficult to dismiss her image from his mind, he had to meet her once more. Why had she come? An absurd question. In the fury of the moment he was beyond clear reasoning. He didn't even ask himself how she had managed to get into the factory; the firm was always advertising for labour, and that was explanation enough. He didn't stop to wonder if any woman could be so completely lacking in pride. He saw her again as a designing little hussy who had somehow guessed at his feelings, and had seized the first opportunity of renewing their acquaintance, confident that this time he would be totally unable to resist her. How had he come to give himself away? he wondered scowlingly. He hadn't known himself until he was on the train. His anger increased as he at last admitted the truth. He'd known it, of course, known on the train how very near he had come, that last evening, to making a fool of himself, but the knowledge had been deliberately pushed into some obscure recess of his mind and he had stubbornly refused to admit it was there at all.

What was the use of pretence now when, even in her soiled overall and with her hair falling untidily about her face, she could stir his heart and set his pulses racing? What sort of a man was he to be attracted to a woman like that?

When had she guessed? he asked himself again. How could he have been such a fool as to reveal what he felt? He remembered again that last evening. She must have known how near he had come to weakening, even though he had been totally unaware of it himself. Surely she guessed that he despised her type, that even if he married her he would still despise her. A sneer curved his lips. She didn't care; it troubled her not at all that she appealed only to his baser instincts. . . . But did she appeal only to his baser instincts? After dwelling on the question for some time he then shirked the answer and speculated instead on what Muriel was thinking at this very moment. Was she waiting expectantly for his summons, or had their meeting damped her confidence? He congratulated himself on that; he remained aloof, impersonal, even while intensely alive to the fact that she was far more attractive now than at any time on the cruise.

Five weeks. . . . Why hadn't she made some move to contact him? But no . . . too clever for that; it would have been too clumsy and brazen a method of approach. He made a practice of visiting each department every six weeks or so; she had waited patiently for him to see her.

And in all probability she now waited for a summons, waited with some pathetic story designed to soften him and make him as putty in her hands. His lips curved again in a sneer. He would send for her, listen to whatever story she had to relate – and then he would send her back to her job with the humiliating knowledge that she'd made the greatest miscalculation of her life.

On entering the office he found Bill Raines seated in a chair by the desk, a cigarette in his mouth, a cup of tea at his elbow. Andrew frowned darkly, he had no wish for company. His one urgent desire was to interview Muriel and go home this afternoon with the sure conviction that she would not return to the factory in the morning. He glanced at his watch; nearly half-past four.

'Hello, Andrew.' Bill grinned cheerfully at him. 'Want some tea? Old sour face brought a full pot, so there's plenty left. Don't know how you put up with that woman around all day – I always choose bright young things for secretaries myself; may as well, when I've to keep looking at 'em. Always having new ones, of course, because they will go off and get married just when you have them nicely trained. All the same, wouldn't have a hag like that about. Shall I ask her for another cup and saucer?'

'I don't want tea, thank you.' Andrew went behind the desk and sat down. 'Don't you ever work?' he said testily, and Bill cast him a sharp and puzzled glance.

'Kath's been over for a few days and I've just taken her to the station. What's eating you? Trouble in the works?'

Andrew hesitated; for some inexplicable reason he felt disinclined to talk about Muriel to Bill. Yet, when he did speak his voice was edged with contempt.

'I've just discovered that Muriel Paterson is working here – in the factory.'

'Muriel?' Bill stared in blank amazement. 'She's actually come here ... good lord!' The inference was plain, and Andrew, forgetful of his own conclusions of a few moments ago, glared at Bill and informed him stiffly that he was of the decided opinion that Muriel's presence here was entirely due to necessity.

A quick grin flashed across Bill's good-humoured face.

'When you came in here you were of the decided opinion that Muriel was still – er – chasing.'

Andrew continued to glare at him, but said nothing. Bill pursed his lips thoughtfully, thinking of the silent train journey after they had left the ship at Southampton.

'She must know that you fell for her, then,' he ventured when Andrew still remained silent. 'How long has she been here?'

'She must know *what*?'

'Oh, come,' said Bill, unabashed by his friend's scowling countenance, 'admit it. That affair was vastly different from the other imitation love affairs you've amused yourself with from time to time.'

Lord! Had he let the whole cursed ship know?

'Are you suggesting I'm in love with the girl?' His tone was rasping, but his anger had gone with a suddenness that startled him. He realized, with a little sense of shock, that his thoughts were a very long way off and he was pinning a spray of mountain flowers on to Muriel's dress. He saw, not the worldly woman whose falseness and affection had so often jarred on him, but a child; a child with a strange, wistful tenderness in her eyes and a blush of sweet confusion on her cheeks. All part of the act, he had more than once told Bill, and Andrew never for a moment doubted it. Nevertheless, it had been those enchanting touches of innocence, of simplicity, and sometimes almost painful shyness, that had been so profoundly irresistable. She had so often been refreshingly young in her ways, so completely without guile, and she could produce, apparently without the slightest effort, the most captivating blush at a compliment or a teasing remark. How old was she? he began to wonder. She had told him her age was nineteen; she looked thirty; he had judged her to be about twenty-five. But a few moments ago, with her hair loose and her complete lack of ornamentation, she didn't look a day over nineteen, and he was sure now that she had told him the truth. He ought to have known she would not lie about her age, for she fully expected to become his wife.

'I'm saying that you didn't escape as heart-whole as you believed you would,' Bill replied, and Andrew frowned sombrely, wondering what good it would do to deny it.

'You appear to have made some very interesting observations,' he said, and Bill laughed.

'Kath went further; she bet me fifty pence there'd be wedding bells. It wasn't fair to take the bet – on account of what I knew – but she insisted.'

A faint curl of his lip portrayed what Andrew thought of Kathleen's presumption. All the same, it proved that she, too, believed he had fallen in love with Muriel. He gave a shrug of disgust. No wonder Muriel had come here; no wonder she was so confident of success. He must have acted on that ship like an overgrown schoolboy with his heart on his sleeve and an infatuated look in his eye. Incredible!

He glanced sharply at Bill expecting to see the familiar grin on his face. Instead, he found him frowning in perplexity.

'It scarcely makes sense,' he commented slowly and thoughtfully. 'Even she must have some pride.'

The 'even she' caused Andrew to stiffen. It was a curious thing that although he could condemn her himself, that although he knew her to be a woman with adventurous designs and shameless instincts, the mere suggestion that Bill thought the same aroused in him a swift desire to defend the girl. Never before the desire to champion a woman; never had he been interested enough in any female to discuss her as he now discussed Muriel with Bill.

She had certainly done something to him . . . and the sooner he could be rid of her the better.

'I'm afraid you'll have to excuse me, Bill,' he apologized, trying to hide his impatience. 'I have some urgent business to attend to.'

'But you've told me nothing yet,' protested Bill. 'How long has she been here? Have you spoken to her?'

'I can't spare the time just now, Bill. I must deal with this matter at once.' He glanced at the clock. Ten minutes to five. Muriel would be going at five.

Bill rose, eyeing him with a mixture of perception and amusement.

'Very well; I shall see you Wednesday night – you do have the tickets for the show?'

Andrew nodded.

'Sorry to be pushing you off like this, but—'

'I understand – perfectly,' said his friend in affable tones. 'I hope the – urgent business doesn't keep you too late at the office.' With that he was gone, leaving Andrew scowling heavily at the closed door.

Muriel entered hesitantly; she felt hot and embarrassed, not merely from her recent encounter with Andrew, but also from the taunts and jeers of the girls with whom she worked. Those taunts still rang in her ears as Andrew's austere secretary announced her and withdrew.

'Handsome, isn't he? Did you fall for him? All the new girls do.'

'Fancy blushing and stammering like that!'

'She's still blushing.'

'Did you see the way she looked at him? Proper smitten, wasn't she?' And each remark brought forth howls of laughter.

Andrew looked up from the papers on his desk and, keeping her standing, said curtly,

'There's no need for me to tell you I'm surprised to find you here, Muriel. I suppose you expected me to send for you?'

'No, I did not,' she returned, and knew by the scornful curve of his mouth that he thought the worst of her, just as she had expected he would.

'Come now, Muriel, I'm not a fool.'

For a moment her eyes blazed; but the little flame of anger died almost at once. In spite of everything, Andrew had given her the happiest hours she had ever known; she would not quarrel with him.

'You think I came here just to – to see you again,' she said quietly and with dignity. 'But it isn't true. I came because I needed the money – I have never gone out to work before, so I had to go where I would receive training. This was the only place.' Speech was very difficult when he was regarding her with such cold indifference, and watching his long, lean fingers tapping the desk with a sort of restless impatience, it seemed impossible that they had ever curled tenderly round hers. It seemed impossible that they had ever touched her at all, or that his arms had ever held her; those enchanted days and nights on the ship might never have existed. He displayed no emotion at her presence, gave no hint of any pleasurable recollections of those lovely, intimate moments that to her had meant everything that was pure and sweet. To him it had all been a careless flirtation – enjoyed at the time, then forgotten for ever. If only she had had more experience. . . . But it still would have happened, she thought despairingly. Yes, even had she known what kind of man he was, even had she known he was going to trample on her love with such ruthless indifference. Love was a thing over which you had no control; it conquered even before you were aware of its attack, and then it left you crushed and broken and wishing you could sleep and sleep and not wake up until you were too old to remember.

'So you needed the money, did you?' Andrew's voice was even and remote. She had the rather vague impression that he had given her words considerable thought. 'I suppose your circumstances have changed since we last met?'

'Yes, they have,' she replied innocently, and then, after a slight hesitation, 'We've never been well-off, I know I might have misled you, but—'

'You never misled me,' he cut in quietly. 'I concluded from the first that your aunt had paid for the trip.'

Muriel bent her head.

'Yes, she did. Cruising is the only holiday she likes, but she had no one to go with and that's why she asked me. I was a sort of . . . companion.'

His lips twitched slightly; he said in a dry voice,

'You didn't spend much time with her.'

She hated his tone, knew that she would hate his expression even more, and kept her head averted. After a while she respectfully inquired the reason for his sending for her.

Andrew stared at her bent head in disgust. So he'd been right; she had ready the pathetic little story of changed circumstances, of her dire need of a job – any job. And what did she expect now? Nothing, he thought with a faint curve of his lips. She was already fully aware that her plan had failed. Tomorrow she would not be here.

'I merely wished to satisfy my curiosity.' There was something unfathomable in the way he said that, and Muriel raised her head sharply. But he appeared to be giving his whole attention to the papers before him. 'You may go now.' He spoke in the impersonal tones of the employer, and after waiting to see if he would raise his eyes to look at her, Muriel turned and walked unsteadily from the room.

CHAPTER FIVE

HER first impulse was to leave the factory, and that evening she made a tentative remark about not liking the work. This was greeted by an astounded silence at first, and then by an onslaught of angry protests from everyone except her brother.

'The work isn't that bad,' Fred snapped. 'I thought you were doing very well.'

'You *can't* leave,' her mother said fretfully. 'However are we to manage without your money?'

'I always said you didn't want work,' Dil put in wrathfully. 'But if you think you're going to sponge on us again then you're very much mistaken!'

'Please don't say any more about it,' Muriel begged at last, making a little gesture of defeat. 'I won't leave.'

'Then why did you talk as though you intended to?' Mrs. Paterson complained. 'It's so terribly worrying.'

'I don't like the work, that's all. But it doesn't matter, I won't leave, so none of you need worry.'

'That reminds me,' Fred said with sudden interest, 'I saw Peter on my way home and he told me that Mr. Burke sent for you today. What did he want?'

'Mr. Burke?' Dil gasped. '*The* Mr. Burke?'

'There's only one. What did he want, Muriel?'

'Oh, nothing much,' she faltered, aware of her sister's narrowed, curious eyes. 'He only wanted to know if I – if I liked my work.'

'If you— Does Mr. Burke usually concern himself with the ragtag and bobtail in his factory?' Dil inquired smoothly of her husband.

'How the dickens should I know?' He turned to Muriel. 'Peter said he spoke to you when he was in the department. Didn't he ask you about your work then?'

'Yes.' She swallowed nervously, wondering how she could extricate herself from this tangle in which she was so rapidly becoming involved. 'He did ask me if I were happy at the factory.'

'And then he sent for you to ask the same thing all over again?' Dil observed with thinly-veiled scepticism. 'He must be an unusually considerate employer.' She paused and then went on evenly, 'Do you remember your odd and unexplained remark about the "bosses" as you called them? It strikes me that you knew this Mr. Burke before you went to work at the factory.'

Noticing Muriel's discomfiture, and sorry that he had broached the subject which had caused it, Fred was about to interrupt when Muriel banged down her knife and fork and turned angrily on her sister.

'Just what are you insinuating?' she demanded.

'Nothing – nothing at all. I'm merely thinking it very odd that a man in Mr. Burke's position should be so interested in one of his factory girls—'

'Dil, be quiet!' Mrs. Paterson interrupted at last. 'Your remarks are disgusting!'

'Why did he send for you?' Dil pursued, ignoring her mother. 'And why are you looking so very uncomfortable? You mentioned, if I remember rightly, Mr. Groves – but there's no such person, so you really meant Mr. Burke, didn't you? Where did you meet him? – that's what's puzzling me.'

Muriel stood up, pale and angry, and feeling sickened by her sister's remarks.

'I refuse to be questioned like this. Mr. Burke sent for me to inquire about my work. You can believe that or not, but it's the only explanation you'll get from me.'

'But, Muriel,' her mother said sharply, 'why all this secrecy? I must admit that you're making it appear you have something to hide.'

'I'm not hiding anything. I've told you, he merely asked about my work.'

Dil began to laugh.

'I can't think how you came to meet him in the first place,' she said, 'but it's clear that you know more about him than you'd have us believe. Play your cards right and you may be an asset to us all yet—'

'I think you've gone mad!' Muriel stood there, white to the lips, her fingers clenched, staring from one to another. Then she turned and fled from the room.

'What have I done that both Andrew and Dil should think me rotten and cheap?' she whispered, her eyes brimming over with tears. 'If only Daddy were here I could tell him everything – but I could never tell them,' and in a sudden abandonment of grief and despair, she flung herself on the bed and wept bitterly into her pillow. But Dil didn't mean what she said, Muriel thought after a little while. She wasn't herself these days; she would be all right again once her baby was born. No, Dil could never really mean the hateful things she said.

The matter was not mentioned again, much to Muriel's surprise, and for the next week or two life was almost placid – something entirely new in the Paterson household.

Dil had actually begun making baby clothes and there were times when, observing her guardedly, Muriel felt convinced she was taking a delight in her task. Occasionally, having finished one of the absurdly small garments, she would hold it up, ostensibly examining it, yet, Muriel suspected, waiting for her family's praise. Muriel found a strange content in helping her; she added all the final touches, sewing on ribbons and bows, all blue, for both Dil and Fred had set their hearts on a boy.

'It's funny how everyone wants their first to be a boy,' Muriel said dreamily one evening as she sat with Dil by the fire, working on a little coat which she was trying to finish before bedtime.

'They're better than girls, that's why,' Dil said emphatically. 'Especially when they grow up. Women are such cats.'

'Oh, how can you say so?' Muriel laughed, half in amusement, half in protest. 'You shouldn't call your own sex cats, Dil.'

'Why not? It's the truth. Take our own family, for instance. Aunt Sarah, she's a cat – and so is Aunt Edith. And what of Christine? Who wants a child that's likely to grow up like her?'

'There's nothing wrong with Christine—'

'Oh, no? You haven't ever crossed her, Muriel, that's why you don't know her. I shall always remember the Christmas Aunt Sarah took pity on the poor relations and invited us over for the day. I had a doll – it wasn't to be compared with Christine's, but for some unknown reason she wanted it. We fought like two tigers over that doll and she'd have scratched my eyes out if I'd let her get near enough. You were a little too young to remember, but whenever I think of Christine I recall the incident of that doll.'

'All children squabble,' Muriel said in defence of her cousin. 'Christine's always been very nice to me.'

'Perhaps. . . .' Dil's eyes narrowed strangely. 'You ever come to have something she wants – then you'll see her in her true colours.'

'I don't suppose I shall ever possess anything she would want,' Muriel returned ruefully.

'No, I guess you're right,' her sister agreed. 'Oh, money! If we had to be poor, why couldn't our relations have been poor, too?'

But Dil's grumbles became less frequent; her quarrels with her husband almost ceased. He had received a wage increase and Muriel felt sure that if they had a house of their own Dil would be content.

Aunt Sarah and Uncle Herbert were celebrating their silver wedding a fortnight before Christmas, and all the family received invitations. Dil would not go, so Fred also refused. Mrs. Paterson declined because, she said, she could not bear to spend an evening in surroundings which would remind her so vividly of all she had given up on her marriage.

'I wouldn't enjoy it at all. As for Derek, I couldn't possibly let him go; he would disgrace us all with his behaviour and his slang. No one would ever believe he went to such a nice school.'

'Nice school?' he echoed with a broad grin. 'We had a riot today.'

'Riot?' Muriel looked dismayed. 'But, Derek—'

'Take no notice of him,' his mother interrupted scathingly. 'That's only another of his fairy tales. Last week it was the spanner.'

'The spanner?' Muriel looked blank.

'Oh, you didn't hear about the spanner that dropped from an aeroplane into the school grounds and missed

Derek's head by inches, did you?' Fred laughed, and Derek had the grace to redden.

'Well, it'd have been jolly exciting if it had,' he returned with a grimace, and then, in order, apparently, to demonstrate just what kind of a school it was to which he had won the much-coveted entry, 'Old Killer Jackson called me a bog-eyed bat yesterday, and all because I put "were" for "where". As though anyone could help a little thing like that! And he often calls us scaleless jellyfish and constipated earwigs—'

'Oh, Derek, you're the limit,' Muriel laughed. 'It's time you stopped this romancing. Have you forgotten how old you are?'

'All right,' he flashed, red with indignation. 'Ask Billy Thomson when he comes here on Saturday! Taffy called *him* the son of a spineless toad the other day— Don't you believe me now?'

'I do not,' she replied, and they all laughed. Derek, speechless with indignation, glared at them all in turn and then buried his head in his Latin book again. They never believed you when you were telling the truth, he thought angrily ... and then remembered the boy who cried wolf.

'*Amo, amas, amat,*' he murmured savagely to himself.

'A what?' said Dil, frowning.

'You wouldn't know a thing about it! It's all to do with *love*!'

Strangely, Dil kept her temper; in fact, she actually seemed amused, and there was a good-humoured smile on her lips as she turned her attention to what her mother was saying.

'We can't all refuse, Muriel – yes, I know what you're going to say; Uncle Herbert didn't come to Father's funeral. But it doesn't matter; we mustn't be spiteful about things like that. I won't have any argument, so you may as well resign yourself.'

Muriel bit her lip; she supposed she would have to do as her mother wished, but she didn't feel very enthusiastic about meeting Christine again just now. She had been so inquisitive about the cruise, so puzzled about Muriel's reticence, that it was certain she would bring the matter up again at the first opportunity. There would be a long evening this time, whereas before – when she had gone to return the clothes Christine had lent her – she had had to leave almost immediately in order to catch her bus. Muriel had timed her visit carefully, so as to avoid her cousin's questioning. On this occasion, however, there would be no escape. If only she had not sent that letter there would have been no need to tell Christine anything. But the letter had revealed so much; it not only told of her love for Andrew, it also contained the very confident, 'I shall be bringing him to see you very soon after we arrive home.'

No wonder Christine had said, 'But, Muriel, you seemed so sure of him when you sent that letter.'

Yes, after only four days she had been sure enough of him to write with complete confidence. She had been sure of herself, too, sure that Andrew was the only man she would ever love. It had all happened so quickly, she realized now; but at the time her love – or rather, their love, as she had so confidently thought then – had developed so smoothly, so naturally, that it seemed she had known Andrew all her life.

Had it happened only four months ago? It seemed more like four years since his light and flippant goodbye had taken that new-found happiness from her heart and left instead this dumb pain which she felt sure would remain with her for ever, no matter how long she might live.

'You can wear one of those dresses Christine gave you,' Mrs. Paterson suggested, breaking into Muriel's unhappy thoughts. 'They were both very nice.'

'Oh, no! I couldn't wear one of those,' she protested. 'I never really liked them.' That was true, of course, but by no means the chief reason for her not wishing to wear one of them.

'What else can you wear?' Dil interposed. 'You know what Aunt Sarah's parties are. You haven't anything else that would be in the least suitable.' She paused for a moment, eyeing her strangely. 'What's the matter with them? You've stuffed them away in a box under the bed as if they were bits of rag—'

'Oh, be quiet!'

Dil looked astonished.

'You needn't snap,' she said in an aggrieved tone. 'I don't know what's come over you this last month or two.'

'I'm sorry.' Muriel bit her lip contritely. 'I'm sorry, Dil,' she said again. 'But it's just that I don't want to wear either of those dresses, that's all.'

'Well, you'll have to wear one,' Mrs. Paterson insisted. 'Choose which it is to be and I'll get it cleaned.'

'I won't wear either of them. They're much too old for me.'

'Old? And how old is Christine?'

'I know there's not a great deal of difference in our ages, but they suit her. I'm going to wear the dress Daddy bought me.'

'That thing!' her mother exclaimed. 'It couldn't have cost one tenth as much as the others!'

'I don't care about cost,' Muriel returned stubbornly, and although her mother argued, it was to no avail. Muriel fetched down the demure little white dress and shook it from its wrappings.

'I don't think it needs cleaning; I haven't worn it much, and I've kept it wrapped in tissue paper.'

'Yes, you would keep that wrapped in tissue paper,' her mother snapped irritably, 'and leave the others pushed away in a dusty trunk. You're far too sentimental, child, and it will get you nowhere. Oh, why can't you be sensible and wear something decent!'

'I intend to wear something decent, Mother,' she replied quietly. 'This one is decent – the others are not. Aunt Edith was right when she said they were disgustingly low-cut.'

'Don't be silly! Christine wore them, and she knows what is fashionable.'

'I've said that they suit Christine, but they don't suit me!'

'You get on my nerves,' her mother said exasperatedly. 'You won't even try to be fashionable. And I'm surprised at you taking any notice of Aunt Edith; she had no dress sense even when she was young.'

But Muriel would not argue further; she pressed the dress and hung it in the wardrobe, a shadow crossing her face as she remembered the pride in her father's eyes when first she had tried it on for him to see.

'You'll have all the boys falling over themselves to dance with you when you wear that,' he had said fondly. 'But don't you go falling for them, my darling, I don't want to lose you yet awhile.'

With a little sob she closed the wardrobe door. It seemed incredible that anyone so kind, so gentle and considerate, could have been so quickly forgotten. Even Derek did not seem to miss his father now.

The following week Peter asked her to work on the Saturday morning – they were behind with an important export order, he said – and she agreed readily, intending to give Dil the extra money towards the pram. Having a little money already saved, she decided to spend the afternoon in Barston and buy a few things for the baby, so she went to work in her best suit, protecting it with a clean overall while she worked. And when, at about a quarter past twelve, she emerged from the cloakroom looking very striking and attractive Peter's eyes widened with appreciation.

'You look very smart this morning, Muriel; got a date?'

She smiled, and gave him a quick, appraising glance. She liked what she saw; for he was a physically fit young man, lithe and athletic-looking with clean-cut features and an attractive smile. His hair was dark brown with lighter tints, and it was brushed back from a wide, intelligent forehead. Fred had said that Peter attracted the girls as honey attracted the bee, and Muriel had already discovered the truth of this. But Peter was clearly not interested in any of the girls working under him. Not interested in any except Muriel. . . .

'No, I'm going shopping, that's all.'

'Will you be in Barston all the afternoon?'

'I don't know . . . yes, I suppose I will; I have to get my lunch first.'

'Then let me meet you later on. We could have tea in town and then go to a show.'

'It's very nice of you to ask me, Peter, but my mother expects me home for tea.' She glanced at her watch. 'I must hurry or I'll miss that twelve-thirty bus.'

'What about tomorrow, then?' he persisted. 'I have a little car; we could go for a run.'

'I'm sorry. I help at home on Sundays.'

'I think you're just making excuses,' he said, keenly disappointed. 'Don't you like me, or is it that you have a boy-friend already?'

'I have no boy-friend, and I like you very much,' she smiled. 'But I really am busy on Sundays.'

'All right.' He shrugged resignedly. 'But if you have no boy-friend there's still hope. I'll see you on Monday.'

'Yes. Goodbye, Peter.'

She arrived at the bus stop breathless, and took her place at the end of the queue. Her foot was on the step when the conductor put out his hand.

'Sorry, miss, there's too many standing already.'

Muriel stepped back on to the pavement and stood uncertainly, wondering whether it would be quicker to walk to the town centre or wait for another bus.

There was a stream of traffic behind the bus, waiting for it to move, and glancing casually at the first car, a new-looking Bentley, she saw Andrew at the wheel. For the briefest moment their eyes met, then Andrew, a heavy frown darkening his face, returned his attention to the road and the car glided softly away. Muriel watched its slow progress behind the bus, telling herself that it was utterly ridiculous to think of his offering her a lift, that she didn't want one. It would be unbearable to sit there beside Andrew. ... 'But he could have nodded,' she whispered, her lips trembling convulsively. 'He could have nodded in recognition.' The tears stung her eyes, threatening to escape on to her cheeks; with a supreme effort she forced them back and began to walk slowly towards the centre of the town. How could he have looked through her as though they were complete strangers? She felt crushed and despised as she raised her head to pick out the car from the congestion of traffic. But it was gone, leaving only the memory of that cold proud face and the sudden frown that had crossed it.

Twenty minutes later she was passing the Midland,

Barston's largest and most luxurious hotel – and there in the entrance, fur-coated and elegant, stood her cousin. There was no chance of passing unobserved, for even as she lowered her head and increased her pace, Christine's soft, husky voice floated to her.

'Muriel!'

She turned, endeavouring to hide her guilt by saying, with affected surprise,

'Hello, Christine, I never expected to see you here!'

'You're quite a stranger, darling. Why haven't you been to see us?'

It was on the tip of Muriel's tongue to remind her that she hadn't been invited to do so, but she refrained.

'I don't go out very much – and you do live rather a long way off, you know.'

'What are you doing now that Uncle Henry is dead? – you sold the shop, I hear?'

'Yes; I'm working. I managed to get a job at—'

'Yes, you must be. But how awful! Are you hating it? – going out to work after having been your own mistress, so to speak? How is the family?'

She wasn't in the least interested, Muriel thought, and for no apparent reason she was remembering again her uncle's excuses when asked to her father's funeral.

'They're all quite well, thank you, Christine. Dil expects her baby any day now.' She looked about her. 'Are you waiting for Aunt Sarah?'

'No—' Christine's face suddenly glowed. 'Do you remember my telling you about a young man I had met?'

'The one you said you were going to marry?' Muriel put in with a faint smile.

'Yes – wasn't it dreadful of me?' Christine chuckled. 'It had always been so easy, you see, and I was sure I could make him crazy about me without the least effort.

That's why I was so confident when I told you about him. But it's been much more difficult than I imagined. Do you know, that until a couple of weeks ago he never gave me more than a cursory glance! I could hardly believe it! However, he has noticed me now and I'm meeting him here in—' She glanced at her watch. 'He ought to be here now; he had some business to attend to after leaving the office, so he may be a little late. We're having lunch at the Midland and then going on to his home; his mother has invited me to dinner.' Her eyes twinkled. 'I hope I impress the old girl.'

'I'm sure your young man's mother will like you,' Muriel said, casting Christine an appraising glance. 'It just couldn't be otherwise.'

'Flatterer!' she laughed, but with obvious gratification. 'Oh, Muriel, I'm so thrilled! You have no idea what it's like to be *really* in love! I've thought I've been in love before, but this is *it*!'

Muriel looked down at her hands; if Christine had forgotten what she had told her then she was glad. But she rather thought her cousin inwardly scoffed at her own love affair, thought she had not been *really* in love. Whichever it was, she felt heartily thankful that she had escaped the awkward questions she had expected at her next meeting with Christine.

'I must go now,' she said. 'I have some shopping to do.'

'Goodbye, darling,' Christine gushed. 'We'll be seeing you at the party?'

'Yes.'

'And, Muriel ...' for the briefest moment she paused, 'I'll keep that promise I made when we were kids. You will be my chief bridesmaid.'

'Are you engaged – oh, I didn't think—'

'No, not yet – but I'm sure it won't be long. Perhaps

I'll have some more to tell you next week when you come to the party. Goodbye, darling, and love to the family.'

'Goodbye, Christine.' Muriel made her way to the pedestrian crossing a few yards farther on; she was just about to cross the road when something made her look back. Christine was moving towards the car that was drawing to a standstill in the forecourt of the hotel and Muriel couldn't resist waiting to get a glimpse of the man who had at last gained her cousin's affections. But that car.... Andrew emerged and her whole body went rigid; she stood frozen to the spot, unable to move even had she wished.

'Andrew ...! It can't be!' She passed a hand over her eyes, shaking her head as though to see more clearly. He had taken her cousin's arm, so only their backs were visible as they passed into the hotel. No mistake; those broad, imperious shoulders she would know anywhere.

Andrew and Christine ... Andrew and Christine.... How long she stood there repeating their names she did not know; her mind and body were too numbed by the shock to be able to think or feel. But it seemed like the measureless aeons of eternity; it seemed she had repeated those two names a million times. Andrew and Christine—

A klaxon awoke her from her stupor; insensibly she must have stepped off the pavement and was dimly aware that she held up the traffic. A taxi driver put his head through the window of his cab.

'Just give the wire when you've finished your day-dreaming, miss. But don't let us hurry you,' he said, and with a tremendous effort she dragged herself to the other side of the street.

Had the events of the past few moments really happened? They seemed so unreal that she felt like a dreamer in a half sleep; she turned swiftly as though expecting to see her cousin standing there still, or stepping forward to meet someone who wasn't driving a black car at all; someone who didn't smile in that particular way, or walk with that particular grace, or tower above everyone else with that air of majestic splendour. In fact, someone who was an absolute stranger to Muriel. . . .

But Christine wasn't there, and Andrew's car was, and Christine's words were ringing in Muriel's ears.

'I'll keep that promise I made when we were kids. You'll be my chief bridesmaid.'

CHAPTER SIX

MURIEL went into the gardens surrounding the Cenotaph and sat down, her shopping forgotten. Andrew and Christine . . . it began all over again. She shivered violently; stupid to have put on a suit, and more stupid still to sit here in the cold. Not a soul except herself in the gardens. . . . Impossible to take her eyes off the building opposite; somewhere behind those red walls Andrew was lunching . . . with Christine. She knew just how he would be looking, thrilling his companion with that indulgent smile on his lips and that teasing light in his eyes. 'And then they'll drive into the country, to Andrew's home.' She was talking quite audibly, but was scarcely aware of it. 'His mother is sure to approve of Christine – perhaps she'll advise Andrew, tell him what a suitable match it would be.' Yes, Christine had just about everything Andrew could desire in a wife: beauty, polish, self-assurance, and, perhaps the most important, she was the only child of a very wealthy man; a man who did a great deal of business with Andrew.

Yes, his mother was certain to approve of Christine. Andrew had shown her a snapshot of his mother, Muriel remembered – a tall, stately woman with her son's arrogant features. But there was a certain something in her eyes seldom seen in his, something which had convinced Muriel that she would find it much easier to forgive than he would.

Muriel found her thoughts racing on to the future. Christine married, on her honeymoon, with babies— 'Oh, why must I torture myself like this!' she cried in anguish. 'I must forget – put them both out of my mind.' But the torture went on, holding her in its cruel grip until, suddenly, she realized she was weeping, that the tears were spilling on to her cheeks and down the front of her blouse. A furtive glance told her that she was still the lone occupant of the gardens, and, bringing out a handkerchief, she wiped her face. Then she rose and went to the gate. Five minutes later, having no recollection of the walk up Market Street, she found herself in the shopping centre. Only then did she catch sight of a clock. Ten minutes past three . . . she must have been sitting in the gardens for over two hours! They had left the hotel and she hadn't noticed. By now they would be at Andrew's home. There were several hours before dinner; perhaps they would go for a long walk together, or perhaps they would just sit cosily by the fire and talk— 'I won't keep on thinking about it, I *won't*!' But even as the whispered words left her lips, a wild tremor of panic swept through her as other, even more dismaying thoughts took possession of her.

The cruise! Now that Andrew and Christine had become so friendly it must enter some time into the conversation. And when it did, Christine would know everything. She would know that Andrew was the man over whom Muriel had made such a complete fool of herself. Muriel fairly writhed with shame and humiliation until, suddenly, it dawned on her that Andrew, too, would find himself in an unspeakably embarrassing position. The thought gave her an unaccountable feeling of hope. Andrew, she felt sure, had never been in an embarrassing position in his life and, try as she would, she couldn't imagine his being in one now. No, he would manage to wriggle out of it, and by so doing, he would be saving Muriel's face, too. Just how he would do this she had no idea, for she could not visualize how the conversation would go once the mention of the cruise had been made. All she could do was dwell wretchedly on the matter the whole week-end, and by the time Monday morning came round she had decided that she must see Andrew and find out what had happened. As soon as she felt reasonably certain that he would have arrived she slipped away from her work and ran swiftly across the yard to the large, newly-built block of offices. Andrew's secretary looked her over with surprised disdain and said curtly that he was engaged.

'Perhaps you would like to leave a message?' she added.

'No – no, I must see him. The matter is very urgent. I'll leave my name and come back later. Will you tell him that Miss Paterson wishes to speak to him on a very important matter?'

She returned at eleven o'clock. Andrew's secretary informed her that he would not be at liberty that day, and he had given her instructions to take a message.

'I can't leave a message,' she said, relief pouring through her at the sure knowledge that the cruise had not yet been mentioned. For if it had, Andrew would see her no matter how busy he might be. 'Will you please tell him that the matter is a personal one?'

Miss Cook eyed her curiously, and opened the door of Andrew's office. In the brief moment before she closed it behind her Muriel saw that he was alone. Her eyes widened. He just didn't wish to see her ... was still under the impression that she was running after him!

'Mr. Burke is sorry, but he's too busy to see you,' Miss Cook said brusquely when she returned.

'I must see him – it's most important—'

'Mr. Burke said that if you persisted I was to tell you that there's absolutely nothing you could wish to see him about.'

'But—'

'I'm sorry, Miss Paterson; I must ask you to leave. Those are my instructions.'

Muriel stared at her incredulously.

'He told you to order me out of the office!'

'I wouldn't put it quite like that, Miss Paterson. Mr. Burke is too busy to see you, that's all.' Her colourless eyes took in every detail of Muriel's slender figure, and Muriel flushed vividly as she read her expression. It was plain that Miss Cook was wondering just what had been going on between her boss and this girl from the factory.

Muriel's eyes flickered at last to the closed door; something in their expression caught Miss Cook's attention and with a swift stride she was at the door, her hand resting determinedly on the knob.

'I'm afraid I have no more time to waste,' she said. 'If this concerns your work you should make your complaint to your foreman. Good morning, Miss Paterson!'

For a moment Muriel stood there, staring at Miss Cook through a sudden mist of tears. Then, with a little shrug of helplessness, she turned and stumbled from the room. Once outside her control gave way, and great sobs shook her frame. The reason for wanting an interview with Andrew seemed no longer important; the only important thing was that he had given that hateful woman instructions to order her out of the office.

The rest of the morning seemed interminable; she prayed for lunch-time, feeling that the break must bring some sort of relief. But it brought none. She wasn't hungry, and at ten minutes past twelve she left the canteen and returned to the workroom. It was clear that Andrew thought she was running after him, but as so many weeks had passed without her making any attempt to see him, she found his conduct this morning inexcusable. He could have granted her an interview if only to see whether or not his suspicions were correct.

She strove to dismiss that humiliating little scene in Miss Cook's office from her mind, but it was replaced by even more unbearable thoughts. She tortured herself by reading the announcement of the engagement, by living through the weeks that followed, and even by going with Andrew and Christine on their honeymoon!

'It must end some time,' she whispered on a choking little sob. 'This couldn't possibly go on for ever.' Yes, time healed everything, so it was said. When they were married this torment would begin to lessen; gradually – very gradually – she would get used to the idea of Andrew and her cousin as husband and wife. She would be able to visit them, if asked, without feeling one tinge of emotion— 'Oh, no, I wouldn't. Not if I live to be a hundred!'

Impatiently she got up from her stool; if she went on like this she would be reduced to a state bordering on insanity. She must put them out of her mind, concentrate on other things ... but what things?

As though in answer to a prayer, Peter came into the room.

'Why, Muriel, what are you doing here? You haven't had your lunch already?'

'I've had a little.' Unconsciously she brushed a quivering hand through her hair, and Peter looked at her frowningly.

'Don't you feel well?'

'Yes, I'm quite well, thank you, Peter.'

'You certainly don't look it,' he said with a touch of anxiety. 'Sit down for a while. Would you like a cup of tea? I'll fetch you one from the canteen.'

How good he was, she thought, comparing him with Andrew.

'You're very kind.' She looked up at him and managed a wan smile. 'But I did have some tea just now.'

Peter brought a stool and sat down, pulling her on to the other one beside him.

'You're unhappy over something,' he said gently. 'Is anything wrong at home?'

'No – why should you ask that?'

'I don't know. I suppose I can't think of any other reason for your unhappiness.'

Did she show it so very plainly, then? With a determined effort she produced a laugh; a poor little laugh it was true. Nevertheless, it was a beginning, and one had to begin somewhere.

'I'm full of self-pity, that's the only trouble with me,' she said, and Peter frowned.

'The job ...? You don't get on with the girls?'

'Oh, I get on with them all right—'

'But you never make any friends.' He shook his head. 'They're not your sort, are they, Muriel? You're not happy here – I wonder if I could get you a transfer.'

'I don't want a transfer. In any case, what else could I do?'

'Don't know, but as a matter of fact I've been trying to think of a suitable position for you for some time.'

'You have?' She stared at him. 'Why?'

He smiled rather wanly and, taking her hand, put it on the bench and covered it with his own.

'You're not naturally dull, my dear, you just don't want to see, that's all. Isn't it obvious to you that I hate your being with these vulgar women?'

She immediately defended them. True, they were not her sort; they liked the kind of jokes that made her blush, they talked about things that caused her to tingle with shame, but a more generous lot of people it would be very hard to find. They helped one another over difficulties; if anything went wrong they were all up in instant defence of the one who had made the mistake, and if any of them happened to be ill there were plenty of volunteers to take her home, even though most of them were on piecework.

'I admit they're a grand lot,' Peter said. 'And they're generous to a fault, but they're not your sort. You'll never fit in here, Muriel.'

'I'm getting used to them, and I'm getting used to the work. I would hate to go anywhere else.'

He noticed the determined line of her chin and allowed the matter to drop for the present. How pale and troubled she looked, he thought, and gave her hand a little squeeze.

'Let me take you to the pictures tonight,' he said, on a strange note of pleading. 'I want to very much,

Muriel.'

There was the merest pause, then a smile flickered. 'Thank you, Peter, I should enjoy that.'

He looked so pleased and surprised that her conscience suddenly smote her. She was flying to Peter in order to escape from her own unhappy thoughts, using him for her own ends. He was too good to be hurt, and there was no doubt that he would be hurt when he found that their friendship could not lead to any definite goal. She saw herself in a new light, and for the next minute or so her meditations were painfully self-accusatory.

'Peter, no – on second thoughts, I don't think—'

'Oh, Muriel, please don't take it back! What made you change your mind so suddenly?'

'I don't know,' she answered lamely. 'But it's better if we don't become – friendly.'

'I see. . . .' His eyes were dark with perception. 'So that's the cause of your unhappiness.'

'What are you—?'

'It's too late to dissemble, my dear,' he said flatly. 'Is he married? – or in love with someone else?'

She hesitated, but only for a moment.

'He's in love with someone else,' and then, urgently, 'You won't say anything to Fred?'

'I wouldn't dream of discussing this with anyone,' he returned, with slight indignation.

'I'm sorry, but you might just have let something slip out.'

A long silence followed, but at last Peter gave her hand another squeeze.

'I can't agree that we mustn't be friends,' he said. 'Let me take you out this evening?'

'You still want to?'

'Yes, I do, Muriel, and,' he added, 'you have no

excuse for refusing. You've as good as told me we can never be more than friends, and I'm willing to take you out on those conditions.'

'Oh, Peter—' Her fingers clasped his in a gesture of gratitude. 'You're so good, so understanding.'

For a brief moment she thought she detected pain in his eyes, but then he seemed to notice her intent gaze and a smile broke over his face.

'You haven't answered me,' he said quietly.

'Are you quite sure?'

'Quite.'

'Very well, then, I'll come.' She looked at him mistily. 'I didn't think it would help to tell anyone, but it has. I feel much better now.'

'You never confide in your family?'

She shook her head.

'They wouldn't understand.'

Peter stood up, pulling her up with him.

'If I can be a good and understanding friend, then that's all I ask,' he told her sincerely. 'Knowing you, I'm not going to make the mistake of saying you'll soon forget this man, but time is a—'

'No, Peter, no! Please – I want to forget him – quickly, very quickly.' She sounded so distracted that on a sudden impulse he put his arms on her shoulders and drew her closer to him . . . and neither of them saw the man who, passing the wide doorway, glanced casually in and then halted abruptly, a heavy frown darkening his face. They did not see him make a movement to enter the building, hesitate, and then, his lips curling contemptuously, turn away and walk briskly across the yard towards the main offices.

'Then let me help you to forget.' There were a dozen questions he wanted to ask, but they would only cause her pain. 'Let me be your friend, Muriel.' She did not speak, and after a little while he put his hand under her chin in a faintly awed manner and turned up her face. He was smiling ruefully as he went on to say that, as the chargehand, he was setting a very bad example. 'This sort of thing is strictly forbidden, you know. Punishable by instant dismissal.'

'What sort of thing?' For a moment she looked blank, then she hastily drew herself away from him, a flush leaping to her cheeks.

'Don't look so distressed,' he said. 'I only wanted to bring a smile.' He reached out and touched her cheek. 'You don't smile very easily, do you, Muriel?'

But she did smile then, and as a thought occurred to her she asked if he had had his lunch. He shook his head.

'Oh, Peter, I've kept you, and there'll be nothing left!'

'That's what you think. I'm a great favourite with Mrs. Turner; she wouldn't see me starve.' He paused. 'Are you all right now? Not feeling quite so miserable?'

'I feel much, much better.'

'Then come and have some lunch with me. You must be hungry.'

'I'm not,' she returned truthfully. 'Besides, I've just remembered that I promised to get a knitting pattern for my sister. I think I have time.'

'You're going to the little paper shop outside the gates?'

'Yes.'

'Then you've plenty of time.'

Crossing the yard in the lunch hour was neither easy nor pleasant, for invariably there was a game of football in progress. Also, one had to keep one's head averted, for a glance in the young men's direction brought forth a volley of impudent whistling. It was because she had her head down that Muriel did not see the ball until it landed, with tremendous force, in the pit of her stomach. She immediately doubled up, winded and gasping with pain. The men all crowded round, apologizing and asking her if she were much hurt.

'No, I'm all right.' Muriel forced herself to straighten up. 'Please go away.'

'I think she should go along to the ambulance room.'

This was greeted by a dead silence, broken only when Muriel tried to walk away.

'Will you be all right?' The young man who spoke to her looked anxious. 'Would you prefer to go to the ambulance room?'

'No, I wouldn't.' Her customary soft voice was sharp and abrupt because she felt so horribly embarrassed at having a dozen or so men around her, and although the pain was excruciating, she made another attempt to walk.

'She's better now – it's crazy to think of sending her to the ambulance room.'

The first young man was not quite satisfied, but when Muriel again assured him that she was all right, he said anxiously,

'You won't say anything about this to anyone – I mean, you won't report it to your foreman?'

'No.'

'You see,' he went on to explain, 'this has happened before – the last time a youngster was hit in the face. Mr. Burke happened to be in the yard and saw it, and he warned us that if anything like that occurred again he wouldn't allow football in the yard.'

'I won't say anything.' Her voice was cracked and husky with pain. Would they never go away and leave her alone?

'Thanks, you're a good sport.'

The others added their thanks and appreciation and then moved away to resume their game. Muriel, suddenly becoming aware of the searing pain in her head, crossed over to the little footpath that ran along the front of the office building. 'Oh, my head,' she gasped, putting a shaky hand to it. 'Why should my head feel funny?'

For a little while she managed to walk on, and then she felt violently sick and knew that, for the present, she could go no farther. Glancing over her shoulder, she discovered that the men had stopped the game again and were watching her anxiously. If she lingered here they would soon be crowding round her again; the entrance to the offices presented a means of escape and without the slightest hesitation she went inside. There was nowhere to sit down so she leant against the wall, feeling more and more light-headed as the moments passed. She couldn't be going to *faint*, she told herself, for she had never fainted in her life. But the dizziness persisted and even when she heard someone approaching along the corridor she found it quite impossible to move. And then everything went black and she slid, very gently, to the floor.

She could never afterwards decide whether she had fainted or not, for although she couldn't see she never remembered actually losing consciousness. In actual fact, it was only a matter of seconds before her eyes fluttered open.

Andrew! Of all people . . . !

For a moment she wished she had dropped dead!

'Feeling better?' He took her arm and helped her up. 'What happened?'

'I was crossing the yard and the b—' She broke off just in time. 'I felt – queer.'

'Queer, eh?' His tone was distinctly sceptical, but,

as Muriel felt her stomach turn over, she was far too concerned with what might suddenly happen to take any notice. 'You'd better come along to the office. Miss Cook hasn't yet gone to her lunch; she will attend to you.'

'Thank you.' His grip on her arm made her wince, and there was an unmistakable roughness in the way he propelled her along the corridor towards his office. Once inside he almost flung her into a chair.

'Miss Cook, Miss Paterson has – er – fainted. Will you let her sit here until she has fully recovered?'

Miss Cook examined Muriel strangely, then her glance flickered towards her employer. The faintest of smiles curved her pale lips as she noticed his wooden expression.

'Very well, Mr. Burke,' she replied tonelessly.

Although feeling horribly sick, Muriel knew she must take advantage of this opportunity and, disregarding Miss Cook's austere and rather frightening presence, she said,

'Mr. Burke, I wanted to tell you that I'm Christine's cousin, and to ask you not to mention that you and I met on the cr—' She stopped, turning in her chair. Andrew no longer stood behind the chair . . . he had left the room.

'Would you like a drink of water?' Miss Cook inquired frigidly.

'No – yes, please— Will Mr. Burke be coming back?'

'He's gone to his lunch.'

Muriel caught her lips sharply between her teeth, but even that could not still their trembling. Andrew must be completely devoid of feeling to go off like that without waiting to see if she was all right. 'He's cruel and heartless, he's an arrogant, conceited snob – and I hate him!' And before she had time to take any of that back her stomach turned a somersault and she leapt from the chair. Miss Cook returned, a glass of water in her hand, just in time to see her wrench open the door and go racing down the corridor as fast as her legs would carry her.

'Well!' Miss Cook was speechless for a moment, staring at the door. '*That's* a little jade if ever there was one! He'll have to be careful, or she'll catch up with him before he's very much older.'

CHAPTER SEVEN

FIVE o'clock at last. Muriel sighed with relief. Within five minutes the workroom was empty except for Peter and herself.

'Half-past seven outside the Paramount,' he said. 'Don't be late if you can help it, Muriel, or we won't see the whole show.'

'I won't be late.'

She hurried across the yard, hoping to catch the first bus. But just before she reached the office building she saw Miss Cook, obviously in a great hurry, emerge from the front entrance and run for her bus. Muriel hesitated, pride urging her to let slip this inviting opportunity. But supposing Andrew was seeing Christine tonight, and supposing the cruise was mentioned and Andrew caught off his guard? Better to warn him if it was at all possible. The car was there at the entrance, so he hadn't yet gone.

Miss Cook's door stood open; stepping inside, Muriel closed it quietly behind her, and only then did she realize Andrew was not alone. His door, too, stood ajar and she heard the voices distinctly. Bill was with him, and while she stood uncertainly by Miss Cook's desk Muriel heard Bill's incredulous protest.

'Swooned at your feet? Andrew, you're joking!'

'Would I joke about a thing like that?' Andrew's tones were brittle and Muriel could almost see the accompanying sneer.

'Was it convincing?'

'The clumsiest performance I ever saw. There she was, waiting by the wall for me to go out to lunch – I always go about twelve-thirty – and as I reached her she slid down, as gently as you please. Wasn't even risking a bruise.' He laughed in a queer little way that suggested he didn't really want to but just couldn't help it.

'How crude; she must have been reading eighteenth-century novels!' They both laughed at that, and Muriel's fists clenched with anger and mortification. She had the almost irrepressible urge to fling wide the door, to hurl herself into the room and tell them both exactly what she thought about them. Instead, she moved swiftly and silently to the door.

Angry tears blurred her vision as she made her way towards the gates. She pictured her unspeakable humiliation when her cousin learned the truth, for Muriel now felt convinced that she must learn it before very long.

If Christine and Andrew happened to discuss holidays Andrew would be bound to mention his cruise ... the *Appenia* in July. Christine then must remark on the coincidence, saying her cousin was on that particular cruise, and even though she knew there had been over a thousand passengers on board, Christine would be sure to ask Andrew if they had met. Andrew, though aware at once of Muriel's silence over the affair, would scarcely deny all knowledge of her. He would probably say they had met casually, but Christine, remembering the description Muriel had given in the letter, would need little imagination to put two and two together.

If only Andrew had let her speak to him, Muriel thought miserably, they could have made it all so simple by his agreeing to keep silent about the affair.

She stepped aside as a car approached – Andrew's car, for there was no other in the yard. She kept her head averted as it passed, but to her dismay it pulled up just ahead of her. The watchman stepped forward, touching his cap respectfully, and took something from Andrew's outstretched hand; the key of the office, probably. Muriel slackened her pace and to her relief the car moved away before it became necessary to pass it. But the yard was well lit and she felt sure that Bill had recognized her, for, glancing up when the car was a reasonable distance away, she saw that he was looking back.

Still talking about her, she surmised, flushing again at the recollection of what she had overheard. She could picture Bill's surprise at the change in her appearance, could imagine his saying, 'Isn't that Muriel? How she's changed!' Which was exactly what he did say, and it brought a sound of derision from his friend.

'You wouldn't expect her to come to a place like this looking like a film star, would you?'

'I didn't mean that exactly. She looks sort of – poor.'

'Always was poor.' Andrew's eyes were on the mirror as if he were trying to catch a last glimpse of the girl under discussion. Watching him closely, Bill noticed the slight twist of the lips ... a mingling of bitterness and disgust. How very plain. ... Bill could not suppress a smile. Andrew, with his lofty assurance and professed knowledge of women, had at last come face to face with the disaster that could result from such rashness and over-confidence. Was he suitably chastened and subdued? Not he. Yet a feeling almost akin to pity rose within Bill as he considered more deeply his friend's position. It must be damnable to find oneself in love with a girl whom one knew to be a conscienceless little gold-digger. ... Bill frowned suddenly, recalling his doubts about Muriel. He had dismissed them at the time, convinced that Andrew with his wider experience had sized her up correctly, but now those doubts recurred with strange intensity.

'In that case,' he said, 'Muriel probably told the truth when she said she came because she needed the money.' He paused. 'What did she do before coming to the factory?'

'Haven't the faintest idea,' replied Andrew with a yawn, and his friend's lips twitched in amusement.

'You know' – there was a marked alteration in Bill's voice now – 'I never understood Muriel, but I had to like her.' Receiving no comment on this, Bill concluded Andrew wished the matter to be dropped. The same thing had happened on the day he had discovered Muriel to be working in the factory. It had happened again the next time they had met when Bill, naturally curious, had put one or two questions to him. Andrew's replies were brief to the point of curtness and Bill had dropped the matter immediately, respecting the unspoken but clearly manifest wish.

Just now in the office, however, inexpressibly disgusted by the girl's 'fainting' performance, Andrew had shown no reluctance to talk about her. Yet Bill felt convinced that beneath the surface something jarred; that Andrew hated every word said against her, and that he bitterly regretted having mentioned her action at all.

'Andrew,' he said at length, in a deeply troubled

tone, 'are you sure you're not doing Muriel an injustice? You remarked just now that she told Miss Cook she had something important to say to you; I do think, as she was so persistent, you might have listened to her.'

Andrew turned his head sharply.

'You're sorry for the girl?'

'I suppose I am,' Bill admitted, thinking of the wan figure they had just passed. 'I was never as hard as you, Andrew,' he added on a rather self-conscious note.

A bitter smile touched his friend's lips; he was not so hard as Bill believed. In fact, after the discovery on Saturday that Muriel still worked in the factory, he had spent the most miserable week-end of his life. He must have misjudged her. She would never have remained unless circumstances forced her to do so.

The past was forgotten; he could not recall what the Muriel Paterson of the cruise even looked like. He saw only the girl in the factory, with her glorious hair and those lovely eyes clouded with unhappiness. A hundred times during the week-end he heard the warning from somewhere in the dim subconsciousness— 'You're a fool', and a hundred times he had dismissed it.

He could send for her and even put her in a better position without falling into danger, he assured himself.

That he loved her he had already freely admitted . . . but he would never marry her. Nevertheless, he could not bear to think of her unhappy and in want.

All most illogical, but for once in his life he was weak, powerless to resist the emotional forces that were driving him.

He knew exactly what he would do. First thing on Monday morning he would send for her, and after discovering the reason for her entering the factory, he would transfer her to a more suitable position where she would work fewer hours and receive a higher salary.

But on entering the office he became assailed by doubts and misgivings, unsure of his own strength and invulnerability.

Supposing she donned that mask of innocence and candour? Could he resist her indefinitely? Should he decide to establish her in the office he would be in daily contact with her – and where else could he put her?

He had been deep in this cross-questioning of his own feelings when his secretary had announced that Muriel was outside and wanted to see him. At once his suspicions returned, though it was fear – yes, he had to admit it was fear – that prompted his refusal to see her. But immediately he had sent her away remorse overwhelmed him and he was about to tell Miss Cook to call her back when he became caught up in a long telephone discussion about a new insulating material the firm's chemists had recently invented. After that he decided to go over to the research department and see the results of the tests for himself. Returning to the office, and deciding to send for Muriel immediately after lunch, he had happened to glance into the building in which she worked. . . .

Why hadn't he dismissed her instantly? All the afternoon the question plagued him. Even with the fainting episode coming barely five minutes after seeing her in another man's arms, he found it impossible to send for her foreman and give orders for her dismissal. What *had* the girl done to him? She must be a witch. He'd heard of such women, luring their victims on by some mysterious spell, causing them to become so infatuated that they lost all power of rational thought. He had never imagined himself as one of those victims!

'You know, Andrew,' Bill was saying, 'that fainting business. ... I can't believe it. I've come to the conclusion that it must have been genuine.'

'At that particular moment? – at that particular spot?' Andrew shook his head. 'That's asking too much, Bill.' Yet even as he spoke he saw Muriel again and realized with a sort of astonished bewilderment that she *had* looked rather shaky and washed-out. Why hadn't he noticed it at the time? he wondered, then immediately recalled that he had been so filled with revulsion and disgust that his one desire was to remove himself from her presence as quickly as he could.

'I tell you it must have been,' Bill insisted, but Andrew made no comment. Having turned into a wide, tree-lined drive in one of the most select parts of Barston, he pulled up before his friend's house. Bill stood by the car for a moment. 'Thanks for the lift,' he said. 'I hope my car's ready tomorrow, I'm lost without it.' He paused. 'Muriel ... I know it's none of my business, but – you're not going to sack her?'

Andrew brushed a hand through his hair in the manner of one harassed to distraction, though his voice sounded quiet and composed when he spoke.

'No, Bill. I'm going to find out what it's all about.'

It was raining hard when Muriel alighted from the bus, and she ran all the way down the street and up the narrow little path leading to the front door of her home.

Her aunt stood shivering in the tiny porch.

'Aunt Edith!' Muriel halted abruptly in surprise. 'Is anything the matter?'

'Matter? – matter?' Aunt Edith prodded the step with her umbrella. 'I don't often inflict my presence on my relations, but when I do decide to pay them a visit they have to be out!'

'I'm so sorry, Aunt Edith. But you didn't let Mother know you were coming, did you?'

'I didn't write, if that's what you mean, but with so many people living in the house I took it for granted someone would be in.' She paused to glare at her niece, and then went on testily, 'Well, well, don't stand there; haven't you a key?'

'Yes.' Muriel was already taking it from her handbag. She unlocked the door, snapped on the light, and when her aunt had entered she closed the door, putting a mat against it. For when the wind was in this particular direction the rain came bubbling under the door and ran in little streams down the narrow passage which served as a hall. 'Dil's gone to a party – a house-warming. One of her friends has just moved into one of the council houses on the new estate. Fred's going there straight from work. Peter's staying late at school, practising for the play they're giving at Christmas, and Mother has gone on a trip to the Opera House with the Elstone Wheelers.'

'The what?' Aunt Edith, in the act of shaking her coat vigorously before placing it on a hanger, paused to regard Muriel in astonishment. 'Are you telling me your mother's taken up cycling?'

'No.' Muriel's face broke with difficulty into a smile, and her aunt's expression underwent a rapid change. 'You can be a member of the club without taking part in the cycling. They have all sorts of entertainments. Last month they had a trip to a large biscuit factory.'

Aunt Edith still watched her with that odd expression, but all she said for the moment was,

'I should have thought your mother could find something better to do with her time and money. And another thing, she ought to be in, with a hot meal waiting. I don't believe in pampering children, but it's a mother's duty to see that her children are properly fed.' They were in the living-room by this time, and Muriel went down on her knees to rake the dead ashes from the grate.

'We are properly fed,' she returned indignantly. 'And Mother hardly ever goes out at night. There'll be something ready in the kitchen.' She blew vigorously and a tiny flame appeared. 'I'll just fetch some coal and then put the kettle on. There'll be a cup of tea ready in less than five minutes.'

When the coal was on, and she was sure the fire would burn without further coaxing, Muriel went into the kitchen to see what her mother had left for her tea. She found a plate of cold meat, and as it was the end of the joint, there was a more generous portion than usual. Putting half of it on to another plate, Muriel found tomatoes and chutney to go with it; then she began cutting the bread. How long would her aunt stay? she wondered. She would hardly go immediately after tea . . . and Muriel could not go out and leave her alone. Why had she come, anyway? As she herself had said, she did not often visit her relations; and when she did it was never in the winter.

'Did you want to see Mother about something important?' ahe asked, realizing that her aunt had come into the kitchen and was standing with the teapot in her hand, looking vaguely about her. 'The tea caddy's over there – that green tin on the shelf.'

The old lady moved to the shelf and reached for the tin.

'I had no particular reason for calling,' she said. 'I had to go into Barston to see my solicitor, so I thought I'd come back this way round and have a look at you all.' Turning, she once again eyed her niece curiously.

'What's the matter? Have you been ill?'

'Ill? No, I'm fine.'

'You certainly don't look fine. Been losing weight; your cheeks are sunken in. I noticed them out there in the hall. What is it?'

'Daddy,' Muriel replied hastily. 'I can't seem to forget him.' She turned, her eyes brimming. 'You have no idea how I miss him, Aunt Edith. He was so – soft, so understanding. I could talk to him – so much easier than I can talk to Mother.'

'What do you want to talk about?' The deep voice was without expression, though the old lady's eyes were wide and alert.

'Nothing – nothing at all. I just tried to explain about Daddy.' With everything on the tray, Muriel picked it up, hastening into the other room, where she found that her aunt had spread the cloth and laid the cutlery. 'Will you bring the tea, and a jug of hot water?' she called over her shoulder. 'Then we have all we need.'

Aunt Edith followed, pouring out the tea before sitting down at the table opposite to her niece. She regarded Muriel in silence for a little while and then said in her usual brusque and direct manner,

'It's that Burke fellow – you've not got over him yet. No, you needn't start protesting and saying you didn't fall in love with him. I know you did! Well, I warned you you'd find yourself in trouble, and you have! It's a case of the biter bit, isn't it? And serve you right! Perhaps next time you'll take heed of someone wiser than yourself! I suppose it's never occurred to you that this is a sort of punishment?'

It had occurred to Muriel, many, many times. But she did not think she had done anything wicked enough to deserve this terrible heartache, this unspeakable emptiness that engulfed her from the moment she woke in the morning until she drifted off into a restless, troubled sleep again at night.

'Yes, Aunt Edith, it has.'

'Then I'm glad to hear it.' Although her tone held its customary sharpness, it contained a strange underlying note which brought Muriel's head up with a jerk. No expression in the faded blue eyes, no relaxing of the small, uncompromising line of the mouth, yet there was a softness somewhere in the tiny, imperious face.

'I know it was very wrong to get an idea like that, Aunt Edith,' she said in a small voice. 'But after I met Andrew it didn't seem important. In fact, the idea seemed to fade from my mind altogether.'

'You'd got your mug then,' the old lady retorted. 'At least, you thought you had.'

'I didn't think of Andrew like that,' she protested. 'I wouldn't have cared if he'd been poor – poorer even than Daddy was.' Her eyes were beseeching; she craved for sympathy and understanding; wanted her aunt to believe that Andrew's money had nothing whatever to do with her feelings towards him. She longed desperately to tell her aunt everything; and that was very strange, for she had always looked upon her as a rather terrifying person, cold, impersonal, and totally without pity. It had always been difficult to believe that she was a mother, and more difficult still to believe that it had taken her several years to get over her husband's death.

'You'd have married him if he had been as poor as your father? – had he asked you, of course?'

Married.... Muriel's lips trembled and her throat tightened with emotion.

'I would,' she returned huskily, and a little silence followed before her aunt spoke again.

'You didn't tell me much about what happened that last evening, Muriel, but the fact of your shirking the final goodbye the following morning revealed a lot. On the train, when I mentioned the young man, you said it had been a lighthearted friendship between you, nothing more – but you were much too emphatic about it. Also, you asked me not to mention him to your family. Had it been so light an affair there was no need for secrecy, but you were afraid that if your family did hear about Andrew they'd guess the truth because you would give yourself away, reveal that you loved him?'

'Yes.'

When her aunt spoke again there was an odd quality of gentleness in her tone.

'Tell me, Muriel, did Andrew Burke ever give you any reason to believe he was serious in his attentions?' She watched her niece closely, recalling her suspicion that Andrew had known exactly what Muriel was planning.

'Yes,' said Muriel after a long hesitation. 'He talked quite often of the future; once said I would love the country where he lived. It's near a forest – and he said I would love the trees in his garden; his grandfather had a passion for trees and brought them from many parts of the world. He asked me if I could skate, because there was a lake in the grounds and when it froze over in the winter all the family skated on it, and friends from round about, too. I can't think what happened, Aunt Edith, I feel sure he meant all those things when he said them.'

Aunt Edith felt sure he had not, but she refrained from saying so. Just as she had expected; he had seen through the girl. Probably met many such money-seeking women in his time, and she felt that in the normal way he would have avoided them like the plague. But for some reason he had chosen to amuse himself with Muriel. It was quite clear that he had gone out of his way to make her feel that the end of the cruise was not to be the end of the friendship. Well, it was entirely her own fault. If she allowed herself to be led by a minx like Christine she deserved all that had come to her. As she glanced again at Muriel's pallid face, however, the old lady's eyes softened. No excuse for Andrew Burke, either. He should have left Muriel alone. He might have decided she needed a lesson, but it was not for him to give her one!

'You must try and forget all about it,' she advised, in the same gentle tone. 'I should have expected you to have less time to think now you're working. Where are you? You wrote saying you'd found work in Barston — are you in a shop?'

'No.' Muriel knew the question must come, and she'd been dreading it. But it had to be answered; there was no fencing round a subject, or cleverly dropping it, not with Aunt Edith. 'I'm working at Burke and Groves — in the Park.'

'You—' Aunt Edith's fork clattered on the plate. 'What did you say?'

'I'm working at Andrew's factory — not in the office or anywhere nice like that, but in the works.' And as her aunt continued to stare at her Muriel went on to explain why she had been forced to go there. Her aunt's pale eyes remained fixed on Muriel's face and she added hastily, 'I suppose you're thinking I could have found work elsewhere, but I couldn't. I tried for weeks and weeks — went all over the town.'

'No.' Her aunt shook her head. 'I'm not thinking you went there after him, but I'll wager Andrew Burke did. You have seen him?'

'Yes, but I didn't really expect to, not for a long time, anyway, for there are thousands of employees. He did think I was running after him; he practically said so.'

'Said so?' The deep voice resumed its sharpness.

'Not in so many words,' Muriel admitted, going on to describe the conversation in Andrew's office. 'Then he just told me to go back to my work,' she added quiveringly. 'He spoke in a curt sort of voice, as if we had never been ... friends; just as though he – he h-hated m-me.'

'Did he now ...?' Aunt Edith seemed to be speaking to herself. 'Acted as though he hated you. I wonder why he should do that?' She toyed for a moment with the bread on her plate, a most odd expression on her face.

Muriel wondered if she had exaggerated; Andrew's tones were brusque and impersonal, but he had displayed no open hostility towards her.

'I can't quite remember how he was. I know I had the impression that he didn't want me anywhere near him.' Her voice broke, but her aunt did not notice. She was frowning in a strangely preoccupied way.

'That was an odd impression to have. You parted friends, you told me?'

'I suppose we did.' Muriel suddenly had some doubts about that.

'Have you seen him since he sent for you to go to his office?'

Muriel hesitated. No use trying to hide anything from her aunt. If Andrew and Christine were to be married she would hear of it shortly in any case, would be invited to the wedding.

Better to tell her now, so that the invitation would not come as a shock.

'I saw him last Saturday, with Christine. They're practically engaged.'

An amazed silence followed. Aunt Edith looked as though she had not heard aright.

'Engaged? Andrew Burke ... and that young hussy!'

'He's the man I told you about – the one Christine had decided she was going to marry.'

'Ah. ... The one who does a great deal of business with her father.' She raised an imperative hand as Muriel would have spoken. 'What gave you the idea they were as friendly as all that?'

'I was speaking to Christine just before he met her, and she said – said I could be her – her bridesmaid. ...' It was a little time before Muriel was able to go on and tell her aunt more about the conversation with her cousin. And then, to her surprise, she found herself relating all that had happened, both on the cruise, and since she had gone to work at the factory.

The story came out in confused, disjointed sentences, but Aunt Edith had no difficulty in reducing the chaos into some sort of order. Almost immediately she knew that Andrew Burke was as much in love with Muriel as she was with him, that his refusal to see her was due entirely to fear.

What an incredibly stupid pair they were!

If he knew half as much about women as he thought he did, he would have seen, after the first five minutes, that Muriel was as inexperienced as a baby! And if she had had an atom of sense she'd know that he wouldn't marry Christine if she were the last woman on earth! They wanted their heads banging together! Her pale lips compressing tightly, Aunt Edith pondered on whether or not she should take a hand in the matter.

'You were a stupid little fool to try and see him,' she

snapped impatiently at last. 'And as for falling in a faint just as he came out of the office—' She grunted in disgust. 'When you felt it coming on why the dickens didn't you put as much distance as possible between you and that office? No wonder he assumed it to be a stunt!'

'But I couldn't walk,' Muriel protested hotly. 'I was in awful pain.'

'Then you should have told him, and given the reason, instead of making a martyr of yourself!'

'I wasn't! I couldn't give the young men away; it just isn't done.'

'Rubbish!' The old woman paused. 'What time did you say you were meeting this other young man?'

'Half-past seven ... but I can put it off. I think he's on the phone, and as he lives in Barston he won't have started out yet. If I hurry....'

'Never mind; my train leaves Barston at eight o'clock. I didn't intend staying long. Can we get a taxi?'

Muriel blinked. Her aunt never took a taxi anywhere!

'A taxi? We can just manage to catch the bus.'

'If we rush out at once, yes. But what about the table, and the pots? Your mother'll have plenty to say if you leave those. You've had enough upsets lately; you're going to be ill if you're not careful— What are you looking at me like that for? Thought I had no heart, eh? Well, I have ... as you shall see!'

As the taxi slid to a standstill one glance towards the clustering lights of the Paramount cinema told Muriel that Peter was already there and waiting. She got out and held the door open.

'Are you quite sure you want to go so early, Aunt Edith?' she said anxiously, peering into the darkness of the taxi. 'I can call the date off ... Peter will understand.'

'Don't be stupid! You know very well I've no intention of allowing you to do so! Run along, and enjoy yourself.' And waving her abruptly away, Aunt Edith told the driver to take her to the station.

'Now, how much do I owe you?' she asked, as he handed her out a few minutes later.

'One pound fifty.'

'What . . . ? You must have reckoned up wrongly!' Digging into the massive black handbag, she produced a pound note and some silver. 'Well?'

'One pound fifty, madam,' he repeated, glancing contemptuously at the faded coat which hung limply from her narrow shoulders, at the formidable brown hat with its large-knobbed hatpins twinkling amongst the feathers, at the tiny, imperious face and the eyes that looked dark now and almost aggressive in the shadow of her hat. 'I call that very reasonable.'

A sigh escaping her, Aunt Edith counted out the exact amount and handed it to him. It was as well, she thought, walking slowly on to the platform, that she had decided against going on to Danemere Lodge. . . .

She felt sure she would see Andrew Burke at her sister's party and she could say all she had to say then. But Muriel must be induced to go, too, and that was not going to be easy, for Muriel was also convinced that Andrew would be there.

'Perhaps they'll announce their engagement at the same time,' Muriel had said, and the old lady had promptly replied with,

'Bunk! His interest in Christine is merely to suit his own ends! That young man's got all his chairs at home, as I suspected the first time I saw him. If you read your newspapers you'd know of the projected electrification of the Saudanian railways; your Uncle Herbert is one of the largest shareholders and Burke's is one of four firms vying for the contract. When Andrew Burke has got what he wants it's *that* to Christine!'

'*That*' was a contemptuous snap of the fingers which had no effect whatever on Muriel. She seemed quite determined to go on torturing herself, refusing to be persuaded that there was nothing between Andrew and her cousin.

Aunt Edith was nearly home before she hit upon a way of ensuring her niece's presence at the party.

'Yes,' she chuckled, collecting up her gloves and her umbrella, 'that should fetch her!'

CHAPTER EIGHT

'MISS COOK, will you have Miss Paterson sent over here at once, please?' Entering the office, Andrew did not wait to take off his coat before giving the order. His secretary stared at him, opened her mouth to speak and closed it again instantly as his brows lifted in a frown of haughty inquiry.

Muriel evinced no surprise as she entered; on the contrary, she walked straight to his desk and spoke first.

'So it's come out – she knows all about us? Well, it's rather late to discuss it now, don't you think?' she said bitterly. 'If it hadn't been for your conceit I could have warned you. You'll agree it would have been far more comfortable for us both had we agreed to be complete strangers?' Muriel spread her hands helplessly. 'There's nothing we can do about it now – unless ...?' She tailed off, aware at last of his odd expression. '*Did* you tell her we had never met?'

Andrew's face was a complete blank.

'Do you mind being a little more explicit?' he asked at last.

'But I am. ... Oh, so you *don't* know?'

'Don't know what?' Andrew tried to remain patient.

'That I'm Christine's—' She stopped, staring at him blankly. 'Then why did you send for me?'

'To find out what you wanted to see me about.' Still he managed to keep the impatience out of his voice.

'Oh, well—' Now that she had to begin at the beginning she found it difficult. Yesterday it had seemed easy, but now she realized she would have to mention the letter, and she could not make him see anything clearly unless she told him what it contained. What a laugh he would have when he learnt that she had written to Christine telling her that she loved him! Nevertheless, it was better to appear a fool before Andrew than appear a fool before them both. 'I'm Christine's cousin,' she said quietly. 'I saw her on Saturday and she told me about your ... friendship; that's why I tried to see you. Christine knows I met someone on the cruise – I wrote to her telling her I would be bringing you – this man – to see her. But I didn't mention your name in the letter—' This was awful! – much worse than anything she had ever imagined! Yet when she continued her voice was surprisingly steady. 'I made a complete fool of myself in that letter; I told her I loved this man, and that he loved me. When I saw her on Saturday, and realized that you and she were almost en— That you were very friendly, you can imagine my feelings. I had to see you, to ask you to pretend we had never met. Will you do this?' she added, an unconscious note of pleading in her voice. 'I don't want her to know it was you – and it will be much more comfortable for you, too, won't it?'

Andrew was leaning forward over his desk, watching her through narrowed eyes, and absorbing every word intently.

'I presume you are speaking of Christine Ridley?' His tones were cold and brittle, and there was a suggestion of a sneer about his lips.

'Yes.'

'And did she give you to understand,' he said in a very soft voice, 'that she and I were practically engaged?'

Muriel's head jerked up; he spoke as though marriage with Christine was the last thing he would dream of!

Yet Christine had been confident; she had said Muriel could be her bridesmaid....

'Did she?' Andrew's voice held a sharp edge of command. 'Answer me, Muriel!'

'Not exactly, but— You're very friendly with her! You were taking her to your home.'

'Christine was one of eight young people invited to dinner on Saturday,' he informed her quietly. 'It was my younger sister's birthday; Mother saw Christine in town a few days ago and invited her to come along. I picked her up in Barston for no other reason than that her father couldn't let her have the car. She wasn't supposed to come until much later.' He paused, noticing that she was shaking her head in bewilderment. 'Several things you've said have amazed me, Muriel, but this statement about Christine amazes me most of all. I've met her at parties; I've dined several times recently at her home, but my visits have been entirely concerned with business. Either you've misunderstood her, or she has taken a good deal too much for granted.'

Muriel was reminded of her aunt's words, and as she looked steadily into Andrew's face she knew he was speaking the truth. Christine *had* taken too much for granted.

But to go as far as mentioning bridesmaids....

Was she so very sure of her own charms, so confident that Andrew would not be able to resist her? Aunt Edith had called her conceited; she always spoke of her disparagingly – and so did Dil. Muriel thought her charming, but could she be wrong and her aunt and sister right? It appeared so, unless Andrew lied. Muriel looked at him again and was once more convinced that he spoke the truth.

'I can't understand it,' was all she could find to say.

'I think I can,' Andrew commented dryly after a pause, but did not go on to explain that he had heard all about Christine Ridley's army of admirers. 'I shall see that she doesn't visit my house again.'

Although well aware that it was unspeakably catty, Muriel could not help feeling a tinge of gladness that Christine was not going to marry Andrew.

After all, she was only human.

'But you will see her sometimes, and the cruise may be mentioned. It was embarrassing enough to have to tell her how – how everything ended; but it would be more embarrassing still if she knew who the man was. You won't tell her we met ... please?'

'I don't think I could deny all knowledge of you, Muriel. It may come out, and then *I* would be in an embarrassing position. If the cruise is ever mentioned I shall say we met casually—'

'No! She'll guess—'

'Nonsense! Why should she?'

'Because I told her everything about you,' Muriel answered desperately. 'I described you in every detail – oh, I *know* she'll guess!'

'Why did you have to tell her everything? Surely it

would have been simpler to have kept silent.'

'I wrote her the letter—'

'Ah, yes, the letter. What woman ever *didn't* write a letter?' He sounded impatient, she thought, but neither mocking nor contemptuous.

'I wrote it after that day in Madeira. ...' Her mouth trembled convulsively, and she half turned her head so that he should not see how the memory wounded her. Why had she said that? she wondered. It scarcely mattered when she wrote the letter. But her words had a queer effect on Andrew; his face went grey, and his voice became unsteady as he said, very slowly,

'After that day in Madeira you wrote and told your cousin that you ... loved me?'

'Oh, please ...!' Muriel moved swiftly to the door. 'I'll go now. Tell Christine we met casually if you like – I can't stop you—'

She had the door open when Andrew caught her hand and pulled her back into the room. For a moment there was silence as both stood staring down at her hand in his.

Andrew's thoughts went back once more to a moment he knew he would never forget. It was then it had happened, he knew it now. And only four days after he had met her! Muriel, too, had fallen in love at the same time ... yes, he thought bitterly, even women of her type could love, apparently ... in their own shallow fashion.

He realized suddenly that he had been in danger of forgetting what she was. He must not forget, not for a moment ... or he would be lost.

Muriel made no attempt to withdraw her hand; she wanted to prolong this thrill of exquisite pain for ever. And she squirmed with inward shame at the knowledge.

'Don't go yet, Muriel.' He deliberately played with fire, he knew, but as he led her unresistingly to a chair and put her into it a strange feeling came over him. He recalled that once before time had seemed to stand still; to stand still for him to think and to learn ... and again he experienced exactly the same thing! 'There's so much I don't understand— Do you realize how different you are from the girl of the cruise!' He had never meant to say anything like that; the words were uttered against his will.

Muriel touched the hand he had held, a dazed expression on her face.

'I had beautiful clothes then....' A hot flush spread to her cheeks as she looked down at her overall. 'They were Christine's.'

'Christine's? Those clothes were Christine's?' He went pale. 'Had you – had you none of your own?'

'None suitable.' Muriel tossed her head defiantly. 'My people are very poor, Mr. Burke, and they couldn't afford to buy me clothes for the cruise; that's why I went to my cousin. She lent me everything – and gave me the evening dresses!— But you can't be interested. May I go now?'

'No.' There was a harassed expression in his eyes as he stood looking down at her. She had been forced to go to her cousin for clothes.... But what of her personality? Did she change that, too, with the clothes? Andrew felt his temper rising. How could he ever have considered himself a competent judge of character when this slip of a girl had him beaten? All his doubts recurred, graver doubts by far than those he had felt on the night he had left her. Could he possibly have made a mistake? A good many of the women he knew had a decided dash of worldliness about them, but that did not necessarily brand them gold-diggers.

All his life he had judged on first impressions, liking or disliking on sight. He had judged Muriel on his first meeting with her; one glance had told him what she was. Now, he felt he should have studied her more carefully as the days went by, for there must have been some reason for his continued doubts and puzzlement.

Andrew turned and sat down at his desk again, a heavy frown crossing his brow. He was making excuses for her simply because she had been obliged to borrow her cousin's clothes; he had remembered only the little traces of innocence, of shyness, and that she had fallen in love with him; he had forgotten those affected mannerisms for which there was no excuse, those over-painted lips and nails, the ostentatious behaviour, the coquetry. No, he had not made a mistake.

'What do you want?' Muriel was staring at him in bewilderment. 'There's no reason for my staying here any longer.'

'You told me that you came here because your circumstances had changed,' he said quietly. 'If you needed work couldn't your uncle have found you a job?'

'I wrote and asked him; but, as I told you, I had no experience of anything. It wasn't fair to ask him in the first place, but my mother thought I should.'

'So he refused to do anything for you?' Andrew's face became grim; he knew Herbert Ridley for a hard-headed businessman, but he had not thought him as unfeeling as this. 'What made it necessary for you to find work? You say your family have always been poor; surely you didn't remain at home?'

'I helped my father in his greengrocer's shop.'

'Your father had a shop?'

'There's nothing to be ashamed of in that!'

'I never suggested there was. Did he have to give it up?'

'He . . . died—' The door opened; Miss Cook entered and said something quietly to Andrew.

'I can't see him now; make another appointment. And will you bring some tea, please.' His lips compressed as he noticed the glance she threw at Muriel. 'Don't forget the sugar.'

Muriel stared at him in astonishment; he did not take sugar . . . but he remembered that she did!

'I don't want any tea.' She rose unsteadily to her feet. 'I want to go.'

'I'm terribly sorry to hear about your father, Muriel. I seem to remember that you spoke of him rather more than the rest of your family. You were very devoted to him, I believe?'

'We were the best of pals.' Her vision was blurred as she looked down at him, but she did not miss the change in his expression. A softness had entered his eyes so reminiscent of the man she had first known that it suddenly became imperative that she should leave. 'My affairs can't be of any interest to you – I don't know why you're asking me all this.' She moved away as she spoke; Andrew said quietly,

'Please sit down, Muriel; Miss Cook won't be a minute.'

'I don't want any tea,' she repeated childishly. 'I—'
'Sit down.'

'I want to go.' Her fists clenched convulsively and she spoke in nervous, high-pitched tones. 'Why are you—?' She tailed off as she caught his expression.

'Muriel,' he said softly, 'I asked you to sit down.' His voice held no more than a hint of mild authority, but to Muriel's overwrought imagination it was harsh and arbitrary. Her nerves had become tensed and strained during the conversation and this was the last straw. Her restraint broke and, putting her hands to her face, she sobbed bitterly into them.

'Why don't you let me go? Can't you see you're making my life a misery!' The words came in a wild rush; she had no idea what she was saying, nor would she have cared very much if she had. 'Even though you were only amusing yourself you did say we would part friends, but this isn't being friendly – it isn't even being human!'

Andrew swallowed a terrible lump in his throat, and he realized he was having the greatest difficulty in remaining where he was.

'I don't think I'm being inhuman, Muriel—'

'No, of course you don't!' she cried. 'Because you're so wicked and heartless! You accused me of coming here just to see you again – oh, yes, you did, so don't trouble to deny it! And you think it's clever to ridicule me, to invent atrocious lies about me and then laugh and joke with your friend about them. But I did *not* "swoon at your feet" – nor have I been reading eighteenth-century novels!'

'You—' Leaning back in his chair, Andrew eyed her narrowly. 'You were listening?'

'I made two attempts to see you yesterday, but one of them was *not* at lunch-time. I came after five, when Miss Cook had gone, and I couldn't help overhearing. You were laughing at me; laughing at your own detestable lies, lies one would only associate with a person like you. I hope – I hope you're pr-proud of y-yourself!'

He felt far from proud of himself, and would have given anything to take back those words.

'I'm sorry you overheard us, Muriel,' he said with sincere regret. 'I see now that I was mistaken about what happened yesterday.'

'You were. I don't know if I fainted, but I did

feel ill, and I came into the offices because of the men in the yard. If you were a little less conceited you'd have known that nobody would resort to anything so – "crude" was the word your friend used.' She turned her head sharply as Miss Cook re-entered the room, hoping she would not notice her tears. When the secretary had gone she dried her eyes and looked at Andrew apologetically.

'I'm sorry; I didn't mean to make a scene – but you should have let me go.'

He felt more than a little shaken as he busied himself with the tea, and quite astonished to find his hands clumsy and unsteady.

'Please sit down, Muriel,' he said gently. 'I'm sure you would like a cup of tea.' He handed it to her as she sat down. 'A biscuit? – no, you never eat between meals, do you?'

Their eyes met fleetingly as she took the cup from him, and then Muriel's were hidden under heavy damp lashes. He read her thoughts, knew she was puzzled by his remembering these things concerning her.

'How long has your father been dead?' he asked after a long silence.

'He died a month after I returned from the cruise; it was very sudden – I would never have gone had I known he had so little time to live.' Her mouth trembled, and a shadow crossed Andrew's dark face.

She spoke the truth, he felt sure of it ... yet how could he reconcile this with the sort of woman he assumed her to be? There *was* something wrong, drastically wrong, and as the conviction was borne upon him he felt inclined to question her openly. On reflection, however, he realized that it would be rather stupid. If her one object in life was to find herself a wealthy husband, she would hardly admit it!

How could he find out more about her? he wondered impatiently, and with a flash of inspiration he thought of her aunt. The old woman's disapproval had been so obvious that he had been extremely puzzled as to why she had brought her niece. Would she enlighten him? He had had no intention of going to the Ridleys' party, but now....

Having finished her tea, Muriel rose to leave.

'Are you going to tell Christine that we ... know each other?'

'I don't know, Muriel, it all depends.'

She shrugged her shoulders helplessly.

'I suppose you'll do exactly as you wish. But there's no need for you to say I worked here, is there?'

'Worked?'

'I'm leaving at the end of the week.'

'Leaving?' He hadn't thought of that.

'Yes.' Muriel blushed, but met his gaze unflinchingly. 'I've just realized that I can't stay, not after what I've been forced to tell you. I do have a little pride, and you will agree that it's only natural that I never want to see you again.' Her colour faded slowly, leaving her very pale, yet dignified and calm.

Andrew bit his lips, and after a moment's hesitation he got up and moved to the other side of the desk.

'I'm sorry about yesterday,' he said in a strangely husky tone. 'I should have seen you. I have no excuse to offer – I did say we would part friends and I haven't acted in a friendly way towards you. I can only apologize again and ... ask you to stay.'

Muriel looked up sharply. No mistaking his tone.

'You sound as though you really do want me to stay,' she gasped in bewilderment. 'Why?'

'Because I know that you can't afford to be out of work.' He moved nearer to her, and she didn't ask her-

127

self why his voice should have taken on that quality of gentleness, for there was room in her mind only for poignant memories. He stood so close that it hurt not to be able to touch him, to rub her cheek against his coat. What sort of a girl was she? she wondered in disgust. He was a cad, a man on whom no self-respecting girl would waste a thought. And yet, although she had had over four months in which to forget him, she was still as much in love with him as ever.

'I can't stay,' she cried. 'I must get away from here – I should never have come in the first place!'

'I don't want you to go,' Andrew said urgently and, almost unconsciously, took her hand. 'Stay – to please me.'

An unaccountable feeling of suspicion swept over her, only to be gone instantly as she caught his expression. Was he really sorry for treating her unjustly yesterday? But he's not sorry for what he did to me at first, she thought. If he would say he's sorry for that I think I could forgive him.

'You have your family to consider,' Andrew went on. 'And there's no reason to believe that it will be any easier to obtain work now than it was before. You would be very foolish to leave without giving the matter more consideration.'

Her family . . . yes, she had forgotten them, and the taunts her sister had repeatedly thrown at her.

'I don't know what do do,' she cried distractedly. 'I don't know whatever to do!'

'Muriel, don't cry—' Before either of them realized it, she was in his arms, her head resting against his coat – just where it longed to be. She felt his heart beating, his cool breath stirring her hair, and for a brief moment she was lost to everything but the surge of wild sweet pain that filled her.

Then she flung herself from him, appalled at her weakness.

'How dare you touch me!' she whispered through whitened lips. 'If you knew how much I despise you – yes, I do, so you needn't look like that! I'm not going to deny that I loved you once – it would be useless after what I've said – but I don't love you now. I hate you! Get that!'

Her poor little effort would have amused him had he not felt so miserable, so utterly wretched ... and all because of the pain in her eyes. Even if he had not made a mistake, even if she had been an adventuress at the time he met her, there was no doubt that she loved him now.

Did anything else matter?

He was dazed by his own question. Was his love for Muriel so strong that he could overlook *anything*? Before he had time to consider, that little scene in the workroom yesterday intruded into his thoughts, and a sudden harshness crept into his eyes, only to give way at once to perplexity as he glanced at her once more.

There must be some explanation, he thought desperately, though his voice was cold as he said,

'Why were you allowing young Thomson to make love to you yesterday? – Yes, I saw you both as I came across the yard.'

Muriel had not recovered from her shame and humiliation; she was filled with a burning desire to hit back, to convince Andrew that she no longer cared; his words were a heaven-sent opportunity and she spoke without thought or hesitation.

'I happen to love him!' she flashed with a defiant toss of her head, and then felt almost frightened by the silence that followed.

'You ... love him!' He spoke in queer, hollow-sound-ing tones, but they were lost on Muriel, for she suddenly remembered what Peter had said about 'that sort of thing' being strictly forbidden in the factory. She felt almost sick with apprehension. Would Peter lose his job?

'I shouldn't have said that – I didn't mean it – it was ... a lie. He wasn't holding me, not really, just touching my shoulders— It wasn't Peter's fault. I was upset because you wouldn't—'

'Never mind,' he cut in harshly, waving a hand to silence her. 'You're being clumsy and totally unconvincing. There's no need for you to worry; I'm not thinking of dismissing either of you. But see that it doesn't happen again; we have certain rules here and they must be obeyed.' The employer now, delivering a stern warning. 'Should there be a next time I shall not be so lenient.' Picking up a pen, he drew some papers towards him. 'I don't think we have anything else to say to each other ... but I advise you not to be too hasty about leaving your job; it may not be easy to find another.'

Although dismissed, Muriel stood staring at him in bewilderment. He looked suddenly very tired – and upset about something. Moreover, he was genuinely concerned at the idea of her being out of work.

Andrew looked up and Muriel hastily drew back a few paces from the desk.

'Thank you very much – about Mr. Thomson, I mean,' she said in a rather subdued voice, and left the room.

Dropping the pen on the blotting-pad, Andrew stared broodingly into space, going over in detail his conversation with Muriel; his perplexity returned as he remembered how she had lain passively in his arms ... as though content to be there.

And immediately afterwards she had told him baldly that she loved someone else! It just didn't make sense...!

His eyes suddenly widened in comprehension. 'What a fool I am,' he murmured, feeling as though a heavy weight had been lifted from his shoulders.

Then why *had* she been in that fellow's arms? he wondered, frowning in puzzlement. 'He was only touching my shoulders,' she had said. 'I was upset because you—'

Because he, Andrew, had refused to see her? Yes, that was what she was about to say when he interrupted her.

Feeling almost lighthearted, he picked up the telephone receiver and within a couple of minutes was speaking to Christine Ridley.

His questions were guarded; he smiled faintly as Christine purred her replies.

Aunt Edith would be at the party.

CHAPTER NINE

'DID you see the baby?' Mrs. Paterson took a casserole from the oven and put it on the table. 'Dil looks well, doesn't she?'

'Yes, and the baby's beautiful,' Muriel returned enthusiastically, bringing an expressive snort from her brother.

'Arthur Blears says all new-born babies are ugly – and he ought to know, because he's just had twins.'

'How clever of him.'

'His mother, you wop!'

'The words that child comes out with,' Mrs. Paterson said in disgust. 'I don't know where he gets them; it certainly isn't from here.'

'That's nothing; old Killer called me the son of a spineless— Do you want to know what you are?'

'No, thank you,' his mother retorted and, turning to Muriel, 'I had a visit from your Aunt Edith today. It was a surprise, I can tell you, for it must have cost her at least fifty pence to break her journey—And you'll never guess why she was going . . . for no other reason than to—'

'Where was she going?' Muriel inquired, pouring herself a cup of tea.

'To Sarah's party – you know she *never* accepts her invitations; won't spend the train fare, the old skinflint. And the only reason she's going tonight is to give someone a good telling off. Did you ever hear of such a thing? Some young man, it is – must have done her a dirty trick at one time or another, but to go to the party to cause a scene. She says she's going to show him up in front of everyone; to tell Sarah and Christine just what sort of person he is— Oh, I hadn't the patience to listen! She has always let her stupid tongue run away with her. Is anything wrong? You look quite pale. Drink your tea while I serve this up.'

'Did . . . she say who it was?' What a silly question! 'But she *can't* cause a scene at a party— Aunt Edith wouldn't do a thing like that!'

'Now you know very well your Aunt Edith would do anything that came into her head. No, she just said it was a man. I don't envy him, for your aunt seemed to have worked herself up into a rare temper. I thought I knew her, but I never realized she could be so vindictive and ill-mannered as to cause trouble at her own sister's silver wedding. Be quick with your tea, I want to clear away early tonight; Mrs. Stanway is coming in for a chat.'

Muriel stood up.

'I won't have it, if you don't mind, Mother,' she said, striving to hide her agitation. 'I – I've decided to go to Aunt Sarah's party, after all.'

'Decided? At this time?' Her mother glanced at the clock. 'Is it just morbid curiosity, or do you think you can prevent your aunt from making a fool of herself?'

'I could try,' Muriel answered through whitened lips.

'Well, you won't succeed. However, I'm glad you're going; you can tell us all about it. Come on, I'll help you to dress.'

'I'll have to take a taxi. Derek, run round to Mr. Wright and ask him to send it across in about ten minutes.'

'All right; but it may be out.'

'It was there when I passed just jow.'

Several times during the journey Muriel felt like turning back, for she felt she must be too late to do anything. 'Oh, why must she meddle? Why can't she mind her own business?' she whispered fiercely. 'Surely she knows it's me she'll be showing up!' Leaning forward, she urged the driver to hurry.

'I'm doing my best, Miss Paterson,' he returned affably. 'One more set of lights and then we can open out.'

Contrary to her expectations, Muriel was by no means the last to arrive. Her aunt, receiving the guests, merely said, 'Hello, Muriel' and turned away again.

No sooner had Muriel handed her coat to the maid, who came up to her, than Aunt Edith spoke from behind.

'Why, Muriel, you said you weren't coming!'

Muriel spun round.

'Aunt Edith . . .! Have you spoken to Andrew?'

Her words came in choked little gasps, and she saw the old lady smile in amusement.

'Not yet. I suppose your mother told you of my intentions?'

'Yes, she did,' Muriel replied with a mixture of anger and relief. 'And you shan't do this – I won't have you meddling in my affairs. I thought you were sympathetic the other night, but I see I was mistaken! You came here to show Andrew up, but you know very well you'd be making a fool of me at the same time—' She broke off, subdued by the old lady's stern expression. 'Please – you won't say anything – not anything at all?' she added entreatingly. 'It's awful enough as it is. I just couldn't bear any more humiliation.'

A long silence ensued before Aunt Edith spoke, and when she did her disappointment was obvious.

'Very well ... but I was looking forward with relish to his discomfiture. Don't look so distracted, child, I've promised, haven't I?'

For some inexplicable reason Muriel felt suspicious. Her aunt was outspoken; at times she was actually rude, but ... Muriel studied her face doubtfully, questioningly.

'I could hardly believe it when Mother told me what you were going to do. Were you really going to make a scene?'

Without batting an eyelid the old lady said, in a voice so grim that her niece was absolutely convinced,

'I intended unmasking him! He's a scoundrel, and I felt that your aunt and uncle ought to know what he did to you. He would have lost that contract, and that should have given you immense satisfaction.'

Should have ... if she had been revengeful, Muriel thought. But she wasn't; on the contrary, she hoped he would get the contract.

'What a fool I am,' she quivered, not realizing she spoke aloud.

'We all are, at times,' her aunt responded, unexpectedly patting her shoulder, 'so don't let it worry you too much. Besides,' she added cryptically, 'things have a way of sorting themselves out. Have you seen anything of the young man since I saw you last?'

'Yes, he sent for me to go to his office.'

'Did he, now?' Aunt Edith's eyes widened in expectation. 'What did he want?'

'He wanted to know why I wanted to speak to him so urgently.'

'Ah!' The old lady smiled with satisfaction. So he had weakened, had he? 'You told him?'

'Yes.'

'I'll bet he got a shock when he knew that the girl he'd been playing fast and loose with was the niece of the man from whom he hoped to obtain a very profitable contract. What did he do? – offer you promotion?'

'He isn't like that,' was Muriel's quick and half angry retort.

'He's a business man.'

'Well, he wouldn't – I don't think he would use those methods.'

'All right.' Aunt Edith dismissed that as unimportant. 'Tell me all that was said.'

Muriel obeyed, omitting only the incident of allowing Andrew to hold her in his arms. Several times her aunt grunted and nodded her head, although she appeared strangely preoccupied.

'So he was anxious that you should not be out of work, eh?' she commented when Muriel had lapsed into silence. 'That's just as—' Whatever she had been going to say was cut short by the appearance of Christine, dazzling and elegant in a gown of red organza.

'Oh, there you are, darling; I've been looking everywhere for you— Good evening, Aunt Edith,' she added with condescending politeness. 'Come on, Muriel, there's someone I want you to meet.' Grabbing her hand, Christine pulled her towards the door. 'I told you about him; I didn't think he was going to be here, but he changed his mind—'

'Because of you, I suppose,' from Aunt Edith caustically as she followed them into the drawing-room. Then noticing Muriel's anguished expression, she whispered, 'No use, my dear, there's no hope of escape.'

Christine was on her toes, looking around her.

'Now where is he? What a crush— Oh, over there; come on.'

Aunt Edith trotted along, too, despite the glance she received from Christine. Andrew, standing by the fire talking to a woman with cropped hair and broad, manly shoulders, turned as Christine spoke, breathing a sigh of relief as his companion walked away.

Christine introduced him to Muriel, wondering at the strangeness of his glance as it flickered over her cousin's slender figure.

'But we *have* met,' he said coolly, extending a hand. Muriel's heart turned a somersault and her hand began to tremble in his. So he did not intend to keep silent. . . . 'Miss Paterson works at the factory – don't you remember me, I spoke to you when I came over your department?' and, turning to Christine, 'How odd that you didn't know.'

'You work for Andrew?' Christine gasped, changing colour. 'But – but you never told me.'

'I started to,' Muriel stammered, conscious of her own swiftly rising colour. 'But we – we went on to talk

136

of something else. I had no idea then that Mr. Burke was — I mean, I had no idea you knew him.' Christine was clearly put out, and in spite of her own discomfiture Muriel could not suppress a smile.

'You should have told me,' Christine almost snapped.

'Does it matter?' Andrew's tone was mocking, his eyes glinting with unveiled contempt as he looked down at her for a long uncomfortable moment. Then his eyes flickered to Aunt Edith. Christine introduced them, her cheeks burning even more hotly as she wondered what Andrew must think of her aunt. The old pinchfist could have bought a new dress for the occasion! Not that Muriel looked much better, she thought, wishing fervently she had not been so eager to show Andrew off to her.

What a disastrous thing that she should be working in the factory; some time during the evening they might get into conversation. . . . It was up to her to see that they didn't. A little while longer and then it would not matter; she would have Andrew where she wanted him. A sudden frown darkened her brow. What was wrong with him? The others had always risen at the first dangling of the bait. Could it be that she was losing her skill? Or perhaps Andrew, being so different from the rest, needed different handling. She had not had much time, she recollected; he would rise before long.

As she watched him her frown deepened. How very odd that he had shown so little surprise on discovering that Muriel was her cousin. . . . And they had met, he said. It seemed rather an odd word to use. Did Andrew *meet* an employee just because he made some casual remark to her? Christine turned sharply to glance at Muriel; her head was downcast, she fidgeted nervously with the folds of her dress. Christine's lips snapped together. Here was some mystery; she would have a quiet word with her cousin later. . . .

The opportunity Andrew had been waiting for came soon after dinner; he found Aunt Edith alone at a small table, watching the dancers. Looking up as he approached, she pointed to a chair.

'Do sit down, Mr. Burke, I've been waiting for you.'

His eyebrows lifted in surprise.

'You knew I wanted to speak to you?'

'You came here for that purpose only,' she said, casting him a perceptive glance. 'Otherwise, why did you change your mind? You weren't coming; Christine said so.' She paused as he sat down, then continued in her usual blunt manner. 'Muriel has told me all that has happened, and it was not difficult to see how you feel about her— No denials, please; it will waste such a lot of time.'

'Did Muriel—?'

'No; she has no idea at all that you're in love with her; stupid creature! Must be blind! Now, Mr. Burke, what do you want to know first?' she added briskly, and for a moment his face was dark. Then a responding grin broke.

'Did *you* come here especially to speak to *me*?'

'I did,' she admitted frankly. 'With two such idiots as you and my niece something had to be done. You can be as outspoken as you like, young man; I mean to be.'

Andrew's eyes wandered round the ballroom until they came to rest on the demure little figure talking to one of Christine's devotees.

'I hardly expected to see Muriel here tonight,' he said musingly.

'Why shouldn't she be here?'

Turning slowly, Andrew directed a level stare at her. 'Mrs. Butterworth, in view of the interesting conclusions you've reached, is an answer necessary?'

She chuckled; her husband would have been delighted with the fellow!

'She came to prevent me making a scene.'

'A scene?' he frowned.

'I called at her home on my way here and told her mother I intended denouncing you openly, letting her relatives know what a scoundrel you are. I knew she'd come scuttling here to stop me.'

'But you had no intention of making a scene!'

'Certainly not,' Aunt Edith responded calmly. 'But it was the only way to get her here. I didn't see how I could make much headway until you'd seen the real Muriel Paterson— Oh, I know you've seen her at work, but that's not the same.'

'And this, I presume,' he said, waving an impatient hand, 'is the real Muriel Paterson?'

'It is ... you don't sound as pleased as you should.'

'Pleased. Do you think I go round amusing myself with girls like that?'

'Conscience-stricken, eh? And so you should be, young man; you've caused my niece a great deal of unhappiness.'

Andrew looked her squarely in the face.

'Shall we come to the point at once, Mrs. Butterworth? You've been speaking to Muriel and have discovered my feelings for her. Because of the discovery, you came here to see me and put things right between us ... correct?' She nodded and he went on, 'You've told me to be outspoken, and I'm going to be just that. Muriel's behaviour on that cruise was disgraceful; she obviously changed her whole personality— Why?'

Aunt Edith hesitated for a brief moment as her gaze rested on Andrew's firm, unrelenting mouth. Just how deep was his love for her niece? she wondered.

Deep enough, she concluded, noticing his expression as his eyes found Muriel again.

'On that cruise, Mr. Burke, Muriel was exactly what you took her for – a brazen little baggage in search of a rich husband.'

Andrew's head jerked round, his face going grey.

'What – what did you s-say?'

'Did you think you were mistaken? But of course you did. However, you were not wrong in your judgment. When I invited Muriel to accompany me on the cruise she thought it a wonderful opportunity of meeting some rich mug who would fall for her looks—'

'Do you know what you're saying?' Andrew interrupted harshly. 'I thought you wished to put things right between us!'

'There was, of course, a reason for her wishing to marry for money,' Aunt Edith continued imperturbably. 'She had the stupidest notion that she could make all her family happy—' Before he could interrupt she went on to tell him everything. His interest was soon held and gradually the grey lines disappeared from his face. 'I'm not making excuses for Muriel,' she added. 'I'm just trying to convince you that she was silly rather than wicked.' Andrew did not speak and she gave him one of her direct looks. She hadn't had her face for nearly seventy years without learning that it inspired confidence. 'I have told you nothing but the truth, Mr. Burke – indeed, there was nothing else I could do.'

For a long while after she had stopped speaking Andrew remained silent; he was watching Christine, an unreadable expression on his face.

'From what you've said, I gather that Christine put the idea into Muriel's head in the first place?'

'Oh, we must not blame Christine,' Aunt Edith returned in an expressionless voice. 'Muriel is old enough to think for herself, to know what she's doing. She was very naughty and deserved a good shaking—'

'Shaking?' Andrew cut in wrathfully. 'If she'd been a sister of mine she'd have received the hiding of her life!'

Aunt Edith grimaced. Well, Muriel wanted him, and if she later discovered she had taken on more than she could manage she would just have to abide by it. For herself, Aunt Edith preferred the docile, even-tempered type of man. Hers had been the quiet road of contentment – no being transported to ecstatic heights, but no painful bumps back to earth again. No twists and turns, no ups and downs; she had always been able to see exactly where she was going. It would never be like that with Muriel.

'I wouldn't marry you for all the tea in China,' she told Andrew bluntly.

'No?'

'You'll develop into a domestic tyrant when you've been married a year or two – when the novelty's worn off.'

'But the novelty won't wear off.' His flash of ill-humour had fizzled out and in its place was a feeling of eager anticipation.

'Bunk! It always wears off—' She spread her hands and grinned at him. 'It's useless for me to tell you that, isn't it? Young people never look into the future. There will come a time,' she went on twinklingly, 'when that glorious hair of Muriel's will be grey – and when you, young man, will have none at all. There'll come a time when the curves become bumps, and the wrinkles spread—'

'Mrs. Butterworth!' Andrew laughingly stopped her. 'Just when I'd decided you were highly romantic!'

'A mistake, Mr. Burke. There is not much romance

in me.' But the pale eyes still twinkled under their sparse white lashes.

'You must have some romance in you,' he returned, rather gently. 'Otherwise. ...' He merely gestured towards the far end of the ballroom.

'Well, she could never have been happy without you; and when I was absolutely sure how you felt about—'

'Did I give myself away on the ship?' he wanted to know. The old lady shook her head.

'I drew my conclusions entirely from what Muriel told me. She must be an idiot not to see it for herself.' She paused. 'You weren't really very clever, were you, to fall in love with a woman like *that*?'

'With the girl underneath it all,' he murmured gravely, and then, with a laugh, 'You know, Mrs Butterworth, I have a feeling I'm going to like having you for an aunt-in-law. We shall get on famously.'

'I sincerely hope so,' she responded with a smile. 'Er – how much longer do you expect to be calling me Mrs. Butterworth?'

'Not a day longer than I can help.'

'Well, I detest celebrations as a rule, but I hope you'll send me an invitation to the wedding.' Aunt Edith paused and then added, 'I should love to see Christine there as chief bridesmaid, but I have a feeling I shall be disappointed.'

'You will,' replied Andrew between his teeth. 'Whatever is Muriel's wish, *I* intend to have a say in that!'

'Christine wouldn't accept an invitation, in any case.'

Andrew was not interested in Christine, so he made no comment. Instead, he looked across at Aunt Edith and said gravely,

'Thank you, Mrs. Butterworth, for coming here tonight.'

'There's no need to thank me,' she said. 'I only hope

I've done the right thing and that you'll both be happy.'

'You need have no doubts of that,' Andrew returned, his smile fading swiftly as Christine came up to the table.

'She's been watching us for some time,' Aunt Edith informed him, *sotto voce*.

'I know.'

'May I sit down?' Without waiting for an answer, Christine pulled out a chair and seated herself beside Andrew. 'You two seem to have a lot to say to one another?' She glanced at them in turn, her eyes narrowed and questioning.

'This is Christine's subtle way of asking us what we were talking about, Mr. Burke,' Aunt Edith said, deriving immense satisfaction from the flush that rose to her niece's cheeks.

'It's no such thing! I haven't the slightest interest in what you were saying!' Christine glared at her aunt. Ill-mannered old bitch, she thought, wondering why she had come. Neither Christine nor her parents had expected her to do so, seeing that the 'free' meal she would get would not cover the cost of her train fare. Aunt Edith invariably considered things like that. She turned to Andrew. 'I came to ask if you wanted a drink?'

'No, thank you, Christine. How about you, Mrs. Butterworth?'

'I am a bit thirsty; perhaps Christine will get me a glass of lemonade?'

'I'll get it. Do you want something, Christine?'

'No, thanks.' Christine's dark eyes followed him almost scowlingly. What was the matter with him? she asked herself again. He was about as responsive as an iceberg! She had tried so hard, but mere dogged persistence was useless against such cool impassivity. With other men she knew where she stood, but Andrew had her completely baffled. He couldn't be as indifferent as he appeared; no man had ever been indifferent to her charms.

Tonight he was even more remote, Christine reluctantly admitted. Previously he had been the perfect companion, polite and charming, and equally attractive whether his mood were grave or gay. She had begun to hope, but now. . . .

She became aware that her aunt was staring at her, and deliberately turned to watch the dancers. How odd that Andrew should sit here with her for so long. What could they have found to talk about? ... Christine's whole body stiffened as her nerves went tight. 'This is Christine's subtle way of asking us what we were talking about. ... ' Hardly what even Aunt Edith would have said to a stranger. ... And he was no stranger to Muriel, either. The three had met somewhere ... and there was only one place—

Andrew was handing Aunt Edith her glass of lemonade; vaguely, Christine was telling herself that there was no need for this jealousy that was surging over her. Andrew did not want Muriel, he had proved it. He had amused himself with her and then, at the end of the voyage, had thrown her off as he would an old coat for which he had no further use. She had been someone with whom to pass the time; she did not count.

The reason for all this secrecy was apparent; Muriel had requested it. Christine's thoughts sped on; she soon realized that in asking Andrew to keep quiet about her knowing him, Muriel must have disclosed at least part of the conversation outside the Midland Hotel. The conversation during which she, Christine, had hinted at an engagement between Andrew and herself!

No wonder Andrew had looked at her with such undisguised contempt earlier in the evening!

Becoming hotter and hotter, Christine rose unsteadily

to her feet, The desire to vent her rage on Muriel was uncontrollable; she murmured a polite excuse and left the table.

CHAPTER TEN

'Why have you brought me up here, Christine?' Muriel stood by the bed studying her cousin's face through the mirror. Christine was by the dressing-table, touching up her lips, and to Muriel there was something sinister in her every movement.

'I told you, I want a nice little chat with you.' She continued to apply the lip pencil. 'Sit down.'

Muriel sat down on the bed, her heart beginning to pound madly against her ribs. And then Christine turned; her nostrils were pinched, her lips drawn back into an ugly line over her teeth.

'How long have you known Andrew?' she asked softly.

'Known?' Muriel strove to regain her composure. Andrew had not displayed a sufficient measure of surprise on discovering her to be Christine's cousin, Muriel had known it at the time, but there was no need for panic, she told herself, raising her clear eyes to meet Christine's. 'I don't know him, not really. He came to my department, just as he said, and—'

'You met once, briefly, before you saw him here tonight?'

Muriel was dumb. Christine played a cat and mouse game with her.

'Yes, Muriel, I know where you met. Did you tell him all I said the other Saturday afternoon?'

'I had to tell him some of it, Christine – I had to when I asked him to keep silent about our having met on the cruise. You must know how I felt when I saw who it was you were meeting. I'm sorry about deceiving you, but if you hadn't taken so much for granted, anticipated something that will never take place—'

'How do you know it will never take place?' Christine cut in savagely.

'Because Andrew doesn't love you.' Muriel was more than a little astonished at the calmness of her voice.

'He told you so?'

'He said you were merely acquaintances— Oh, Christine, why did you talk of bridesmaids? It was all so stupid!'

Christine moved nearer to the bed.

'If you're not very careful, Muriel,' she threatened, 'I'll slap your face.'

'I think I'd better go.' Muriel rose and made a movement towards the door. Snatching at her arm, Christine swung her round again, pressing her fingers into Muriel's flesh.

'Christine! You're hurting me!'

Released, Muriel stared at the little bruise appearing on her wrist, then looked at Christine in the manner of one dazed by an unpleasant dream.

'Dil said I would see you in your true colours,' she murmured, almost inaudibly, 'if I had something you wanted...'

'And what makes you think you have something I want?' Christine's voice was suddenly shrill and metallic. 'Are you trying to tell me that Andrew loves you?'

'Don't be silly, Christine. You know very well how he treated me.'

'But he treated you in a most friendly way tonight; there didn't appear to be any antagonism between you. Perhaps it was all dissolved by the laugh you had at my expense?'

'Laugh?'

'When you told Andrew what I said; that would appeal irresistibly to his particular sense of humour.'

'We didn't laugh at you, Christine,' Muriel rejoined quietly. 'But if Andrew found it amusing it's entirely your own fault.'

For a long moment Christine regarded her cousin with undisguised hatred, for what she had said was true. She, Christine, had anticipated something that would never now take place . . . but it might have done had Muriel held her tongue.

'You're a spiteful little cat, Muriel—'

'I am not! How was I to know it was all lies? I believed every word you said; I thought you were going to marry Andrew, and I felt I couldn't bear it if you knew he was the man *I* had fallen in love with. You would have felt the same, done the same, had our positions been reversed.'

'And now you think our positions are reversed?— What a hope, Muriel! You've wrecked my chances with Andrew, but if I can't have him, I'll take good care you don't, either!'

'You don't know what you're talking about,' Muriel said, her face as white as her dress. 'Andrew didn't fall in love with me on the cruise, so he's hardly likely to find me attractive now.'

Christine was not sure, and she tried to find some shadow of reason for her fears regarding Andrew's attitude towards Muriel. Without doubt he had wanted to spare her embarrassment . . . had gone to the lengths of lying in order to do so. True, he hadn't actually said they had not met on the cruise, but it was the same thing.

Then there was the way in which he had regarded

Muriel when shaking hands with her. Unquestionably there was a deeper meaning in his eyes than was revealed on the surface. *Did* he find her more attractive now than when he had first met her? Could it be that he was one of those men who preferred the quiet, unsophisticated type?

'What happened after you told Andrew all about me? How did the conversation end?' Christine watched her cousin intently, waiting for her reply.

'I don't think it's important—'

'You'll answer me, for all that!'

'I told him I was thinking of leaving the factory.'

'What was his reaction?'

'He . . . didn't want me to leave.' Again Muriel was remembering Andrew's anxiety, and for some quite uncomprehensible reason her heartbeats began to quicken.

'I see . . .'

'It was only because he knew I couldn't afford to be out of work,' Muriel put in hastily.

Why should he care? . . . unless he loved her. . . .

'You will do what you intended,' Christine said viciously. 'You will leave the factory! – you have left. You will not go in tomorrow – understand?'

The angry colour surged into Muriel's cheeks; her head went up in defiance.

'I don't understand, Christine! I shall *not* leave!'

'Oh, yes, you will!' Christine moved closer, her face livid, her hands clenched convulsively. 'Because if you don't, I shall tell Andrew all about that adventurous little design of yours! You've had your say, you've filled him with contempt for me, so this is only tit for tat!'

Muriel recoiled from her, Dil's words again piercing her brain. Christine really thought that Andrew was in love with her; she had convinced herself that Muriel possessed what she wanted ... and she was revealing the real person behind the girl Muriel had foolishly looked up to and admired so much.

'It doesn't matter in the least what Andrew's opinion of me may be,' she said, knowing full well that she did not mean it. 'I don't intend to leave my job, Christine.'

'Very well; I shall tell him tonight!'

'No, not tonight!' The words were out before she could stop them. 'I – I—' She stretched out her hands in a pleading gesture. 'You don't mean this, Christine; you're angry and disappointed because Andrew doesn't love you, but you wouldn't stoop to a thing like that; it wouldn't do you any good—'

'Are you going to leave the factory?'

'He doesn't love me— Oh, how can I convince you?'

'Are you going to leave?'

'I can't afford to be out of work— Christine, I beg of you—' Muriel broke off, her brow creasing in puzzlement as it occurred to her that it was very odd that her cousin should be offering her an alternative at all.

'Why are you giving me a chance? Why don't you go down and tell him now? You would be sure, then, that he wouldn't want even to speak to me again.'

'I'd rather hold my trump card.' Christine paused and then went on slowly and evenly, 'It's clear that Andrew hasn't yet declared his love for you – perhaps he doesn't love you at all—'

'In that case, I should be giving up my job for nothing!'

'If he does love you, however,' Christine went on, ignoring the interruption, 'he'll find you and tell you so, even though you've left the factory. And when he does tell you he loves you and asks you to marry him, you'll have no alternative but to refuse him—' She paused to let that sink in, an ugly smile curving her lips. 'You'll have to refuse him, Muriel ... because of what I could tell him.'

For a long while Muriel stared at her unbelievingly as the full significance of her words became clear.

Christine actually wanted Andrew to declare his love; to ask her to marry him! She wanted Muriel to discover that he loved her. . . .

'I can't believe anyone could be so wicked!' she gasped, but no blush of shame leapt to her cousin's cheeks.

'I see you understand me. If I were to tell him everything now you would never discover whether he loves you or not; and if he does, I'd much rather you knew.'

So that the pain of refusing him would be almost more than she could bear, Muriel thought, unable to speak for the feeling of utter loathing that engulfed her.

'I suppose you're thinking that I can't hold my trump card and play it,' Christine went on. 'But make no mistake, Muriel; I may *prefer* to hold my card, but if you don't promise to leave the factory I shall go downstairs now and tell Andrew just what sort of a girl you are.'

'Why do you want me to leave? I've told you I can't afford to be out of work.'

'That's the reason. . . .' Turning away, Christine picked up her bag and walked to the door. 'I'm making sure you receive *some* punishment for what you've done to me. Well? I can't wait all night!'

'You're just doing this so that I'll be out of work? – so that I'll have no money?' By this time Muriel would have believed anything of her cousin, yet her eyes were incredulous.

'I've said I can't wait all night, Muriel.' Christine spoke very softly now, but with open impatience.

'Very well, I really have no choice, have I?' Muriel swept past her cousin and ran down the stairs.

She had a choice, she could let Christine carry out her threat and tell Andrew tonight. It would mean that Muriel would still have her job, for Andrew could not sack her for nothing.

'It really can't make any difference if he knows,' she whispered, making for the cloakroom with the intention of slipping away unseen. 'And yet I don't want him to—'

'Hello, so there you are; I've been looking for you, to ask you to dance.'

Muriel spun round to face Andrew, putting a hand on the knob of the cloakroom door as though for support.

'To – to d-dance?'

'Yes.' A sudden frown crossed his brow as he noticed her almost deathly pallor. 'Where have you been, Muriel? I thought you were dancing, but you seemed to disappear all at once.'

In a rather dazed sort of way she realized that he must have been keeping her under observation.

'Christine wanted to speak to me,' she quivered. 'After all my trouble . . . she knows.'

'Your aunt rather thought she had guessed.' Andrew stopped, his eyes kindling angrily. 'How did you get those bruises?'

'Bruises? Oh, I—' Hastily she put her hand behind her back. 'I knocked myself.'

'Knocked yourself, eh?' A close inspection of her face convinced him that her nerves were taut almost to breaking point. 'Were you going home? You were going in there?'

'Yes.'

'Then get your things,' Andrew said with quiet authority. 'I'll take you home in the car.'

'You take me home?' Muriel's eyes widened; she was suddenly reminded of what Christine had said. 'Why should you offer to take me home?'

A faint smile touched his lips, but he wisely refrained from saying too much.

'You look so tired, Muriel, and it's quite obvious that Christine has upset you. Also, your Aunt Edith was rather worried about you, and asked me to see you home.'

'I'd rather get the bus,' she said. 'It's very kind of you, but—'

'Don't be stubborn, there's a good girl,' Andrew cut in quietly. 'If we stand here arguing we're bound to attract attention.'

'But I don't want to go with you. . . .' Muriel tailed off weakly. Judging by his expression Andrew was determined to have his own way. He had some reason for it, she supposed, but was not interested. She felt too tired and miserable to care; her one urgent desire was to get home as quickly as possible and go to bed. 'Very well, I won't be many minutes.'

'I'll be saying good night to your aunt and uncle. You mustn't leave without doing so, Muriel.'

'No, I won't.'

It was no use pretending that there was nothing strange in Andrew's action or his attitude towards her, Muriel mused as the car sped smoothly along the wide road. Her mind began to dwell again on what her cousin had said, and it was some moments before she realized that, the main road having been left behind, they were driving at a much reduced speed along the edge of what appeared to be a large lake. Muriel sat bolt upright in the car.

'Where – where is this?' she gasped in a trembling little voice. 'We're on the wrong road.'

'There's no need to be frightened, Muriel,' Andrew said gently, bringing the car to a standstill on the grass verge. 'I made this little detour because it's quite early ... and because I want to talk to you.'

He was speaking so quietly, so reassuringly. It was incredible, but Muriel knew he was going to propose to her!

'Take me home – I don't want to listen to anything you have to say! If you don't start the car up at once I'll get out and walk!'

Reaching for her hand, he said with an odd mixture of anger and gentleness,

'What has Christine been saying to you?'

'Nothing of importance— Are you going to take me home?'

'Not yet.'

'Let me go!' Muriel made a futile effort to free herself.

'I had a long talk with Aunt Edith tonight—'

'*Please* let me go!'

'She told me all about that little adventuress design of yours on the cruise.'

Muriel's struggles ceased abruptly.

'Aunt Edith told you ... everything?'

'Everything.'

'But – but—' In that case, he ought not to be speaking in this gentle tone, or holding her hand; he ought not to have offered to take her home at all. 'Is that what you want to talk about?'

'I think the least said about that the better. Your aunt said you were very naughty, and I heartily agree with her.' Although his voice held a hint of censure, it still kept its gentleness, and Muriel twisted round in her seat, scanning his face in the moonlight.

'You don't sound as though— Don't you think it was very . . . dreadful?'

'Your aunt convinced me that you had been more foolish than wicked,' Andrew replied calmly, and, after a slight pause, 'We both have a little forgiving to do, Muriel, before we can put everything right between us.'

'Put everything right? . . .' Muriel trembled from head to foot. 'Andrew, what are you saying to me?'

'I'm saying – rather clumsily, I'm afraid – that I love you.'

'You never said that to me on the ship. . . .' The placid calm of the lake, silvered and shimmering in the light of a young moon, reminded her of the sea. 'You can't mean it— Oh, Aunt Edith can't have told you the whole!'

'I think she did, Muriel. I do mean it.' Andrew's voice took on a note of infinite tenderness. 'I want you for my wife.'

A profound silence followed his words; vaguely Muriel remembered that she had come to the party to prevent her aunt causing a scene, expecting either to be totally ignored by Andrew, or at best, treated with cool indifference. Instead, he was asking her to be his wife.

'I can't think clearly – I didn't expect—' She raised her lovely eyes, revealing their unnatural brightness. 'Is it true?' she whispered. 'Is it really true?' But how could she doubt that look in his eyes? Here was something she had never seen before.

Unresistingly she let him take her in his arms, lifting her face for his kiss, and for a long moment there was again silence in the car. At last Muriel drew away from him.

'But when . . . ?'

'At precisely the same moment as you, my dearest: when I pinned a spray of mountain flowers on to your dress.'

'Madeira? But—' Her eyes widened comprehendingly. 'You've been fighting it? You didn't really want to fall in love with me?'

'I didn't want to marry the type of girl I believed you to be,' Andrew admitted frankly. 'I thought you were exactly what you appeared to be, a good-time girl ... and that was not the sort of girl I had imagined I would one day fall in love with.'

'You like me better as I am?' Muriel looked at him in surprise. 'You don't like glamorous women?'

'Isn't it obvious that I like you better as you are?'

'Yes ... yes, of course it is. You see, I thought you liked me to be poised and sophisticated; I was determined to keep it up for ever—'

'Your aunt explained all that; she also explained why you wanted to marry a wealthy man. Tell me, my silly little goose, just when were you going to ask your husband for all that money? On your wedding night, when you could be sure he'd be in a generous mood?'

'I never really thought about it— Oh, Andrew, it isn't anything to laugh about!'

'All right, I won't laugh. I'll kiss you instead. . . .'

'Andrew,' she said when he had released her, 'if I hadn't been like that – if I'd been as I am now ... ?'

'I'd probably have asked you to marry me before the first week was out.' He gazed at her with an admonishing expression. 'As it was, I thought it would be amusing to flirt with you, to make you feel you had me safely— Oh, dash it, darling, don't let's talk about it any more! Say you forgive me and then we can begin all over again.'

'There's nothing for *me* to forgive!'

'Oh, yes, there is. I was bent on mischief from the start. I should have left you alone; instead, I caused you months of unhappiness.'

'I'm glad you didn't leave me alone, Andrew.'

'Darling....' He drew her head on to his breast. 'Does that mean I'm forgiven?'

'But I deserved it all—'

'Am I?'

'Yes, if you insist on my saying it,' she whispered, 'but I still think—'

'Thank you, sweetheart. I'll make you forget these past months. If it's any consolation to you, I've also found them pretty grim.'

'You're much too good for me,' she quivered. 'I don't deserve—'

'Never let me hear you say that again!' Andrew cut her short abruptly. 'Never, understand?'

'But you seem to think I'm perfect, and I'm not – not even a little perfect.'

'There's no such thing as a "little" perfect; one is perfect or one is not.'

'Then I'm not.'

'You are.'

'I'm not—'

'Don't argue with your boss,' he interrupted with mock sternness. 'You can argue as much as you like with your husband, but while I'm still your boss I'm going to make the most of my superior position.'

Which reminded Muriel that she had promised her cousin she would not go to the factory again. Would Christine believe that Andrew knew all? Obviously she thought he would find it impossible to forgive her. Maybe he would have found it impossible had he heard the story from Christine instead of Aunt Edith. Dear

Aunt Edith; she must have guessed—

'Why did Aunt Edith tell you everything, Andrew? Did she have some idea that you loved me?'

'Yes. She came here especially to see me and straighten things out between us; incidentally, I came to see her.'

'About me?'

'I felt there was such a lot I didn't understand. I wanted desperately to discover I'd made a mistake about you.'

'Oh, Andrew!' Muriel snuggled against him, stopping herself, just in time, from saying once again that she was not worthy of him. 'Aunt Edith told my mother that she was going to show you up in front of Aunt Sarah and Uncle Herbert; she said they ought to know – to know—' She broke off, and Andrew finished laughingly,

'Just what sort of a man I am.'

'Isn't she false!'

'She's a dear. She had to bring you to the party tonight for, she said, she didn't think she could make much headway until I had seen you as you really are ... sweet and unsophisticated— Well, don't blush like that my darling, you must get used to compliments, for you'll hear them regularly from now on.' Pausing for a moment, he added, without much expression, 'Have we cleared everything up now?'

'Yes ... I think so.'

Another pause.

'You wouldn't like to tell me what your cousin said to you?' He was passing a thumb over her wrist; the action convinced Muriel that he had a very good idea what Christine had been saying to her, so there was no point in trying to hide from him her cousin's true character. Besides, Muriel felt sure Christine would not believe that Andrew knew the truth, that she would carry out her threat and tell him herself.

'She said that if I . . . accepted you she would— Oh, I never said you loved me, Andrew!' she added hastily. 'On the contrary, I did my best to convince her that you didn't. Please don't think—'

'I don't, my dear. So Christine had an idea I would ask you to marry me?'

'I don't know why she should have thought so. I did say you seemed anxious that I shouldn't leave my job, but—'

'It doesn't matter.' Andrew's voice was suddenly grim. 'So she threatened to come to me, did she? Well, I'll be waiting for her!'

'Perhaps she won't come; perhaps she'll believe me when I tell her you already know, that Aunt Edith told you.'

'Personally, I don't think she'll believe either you or your aunt – that is supposing she goes to your aunt, which I very much doubt. However, you needn't worry your head about it; Christine will get more than she bargains for if she comes tale-carrying to me.'

'She thinks that, even if you do love me, you'll never forgive a thing like that.' Muriel paused, looking at him oddly from under her lashes. 'When I first met you *I* thought you were the hard, unforgiving type of man.'

'Did you, Muriel? Well, you were right in a way. There are some things I can't forgive, no matter how I try.'

'I hope I won't ever do any of those things,' she returned fervently, pressing closer to him.

'You won't.' He kissed her cheek. 'When are you going to marry me, my love?'

'When would *you* like it to be?' Muriel asked shyly.

'Tomorrow,' was the prompt rejoinder, and they both laughed.

'Do you like June?' after a thoughtful silence.

'I do, but not for weddings — not ours, that is,' he replied in tones of mild inflexibility. 'How about next month?'

'I can't argue with my boss.' A mischievous smile curved her lips. 'I'll marry you next month ... sir.'

'Say that again and I'll inflict a severe punishment.'

'What?'

'Twenty kisses.'

'Sir!'

Andrew laughed and switched on the dash light to look at the clock.

'Punishment postponed,' he said. 'It's late and we haven't yet discussed your new job.'

'New job?'

'You didn't think I would let you stay there, did you? I'm transferring you to the costing department.'

'But I don't know a thing about costing!'

'Never mind. How much are you getting at present?' And when she told him, 'We'll double it.'

'Oh, Andrew, no! I'll be a dead loss to the firm as it is.'

'We won't go bankrupt,' he said quizzically.

'Please be serious. I'll take the job if you insist, but at my present salary.'

'You'll take the job, my sweet, at the salary I stipulate.' Andrew spoke quietly enough, but one glance at his firm-set lips told Muriel that further argument was useless.

'Very well, Andrew,' she agreed reluctantly. 'But I know I won't earn my money.'

Ignoring this, Andrew told her to be at his office at eight-thirty the following morning when he would take her along to see Mr. Pickard, who was in charge of the costing department. Then, frowning, he suddenly changed the subject.

'What did you mean by telling me you loved that fellow Thomson?'

Muriel started, the colour surging into her face.

'It wasn't true—'

'Obviously it wasn't true; but you gave me a nasty few minutes. Is he in love with you?'

'Yes.' Muriel bit her lip. Peter was going to be hurt when he learnt she was going to be married. 'But he knows I love someone else.'

'You told him?'

'I didn't tell him it was you . . . but that was why he was holding me; I was upset because Miss Cook told me you wouldn't speak to me.'

'I thought it was that. I'm sorry, darling; my conduct was inexcusable.' He took her to him and she nestled placidly in his arms. She could feel his heart beating against her breast, the kiss-like touch of his lips on her hair, and a quiver of ecstasy shot through her.

'Beloved, you're trembling. What is it?'

'Happiness,' she replied briefly.

There was a moment's silence before Andrew gently took her face in his hands. His eyes were very tender, but very serious, too.

'You're placing your life's happiness in my keeping. Do you realize that, Muriel?'

'But of course.' Her gaze was childishly trusting. 'You are my life's happiness.'

'It's a sobering thought,' he murmured, as though speaking to himself. 'You will never regret it, my dear. From this moment on you are my sacred responsibility.'

'Oh, I never imagined I'd be going home tonight

feeling so deliriously happy. I'm sure I'll wake up tomorrow and find it's all a dream!'

'A dream that will last for the rest of your life, then,' he said, watching the glow of happy confidence in her lovely eyes. 'I'm very much afraid, my sweet. . . .' He glanced significantly at the clock.

'Yes.' Reluctantly, Muriel freed herself from his embrace. 'We really must go.'

CHAPTER ELEVEN

ANDREW was just turning from the telephone as Muriel entered his office the following morning. He was obviously amused about something that had been said, but the smile was wiped from his face as he noticed the expression on hers.

'Now what?' he said abruptly. 'Has your mother refused her consent to our marriage?'

Muriel turned from him with starting tears and trembling lips.

'I didn't tell her— Oh, Andrew, we can't be married yet, not for a very long time!'

'Indeed? Why?'

'Dil and Fred have got a house. A man Fred works with is going abroad and he's letting them have his.' There was no need for further explanation; Muriel had told Andrew the previous night about Dil and Fred sharing the household expenses.

'How long do you expect me to wait?' Andrew inquired in a strangely untroubled tone which brought Muriel's head round with a jerk.

'I don't know . . . it will be years before Derek is earning any money.' She had expected him to raise objections, perhaps even be angry; instead, he was smiling at her in the most tender, reassuring way. 'So you don't mind waiting, then?'

'I have no intention of waiting,' he replied with promptitude. 'I'm afraid you don't know me very well yet, my love.' He paused in thought, a slight frown on his brow. 'Perhaps your mother would be embarrassed if I made her an allowance.... No, you must do it – out of your own.'

'But I can't let you keep my mother!'

'I'm not waiting years for you, Muriel,' Andrew said with quiet determination. 'Not even months. Don't you want to marry me?'

'You know very well I do. But everything is so difficult.'

'On the contrary, it's all very simple. Now take that look of abject misery off your face and give me a smile.' Seeing that she was about to make further protests, Andrew took her in his arms, and for the next few moments he was doing just what was 'strictly forbidden' in the factory. Then he held her away from him. 'That was an order— Where's the smile I asked for?'

Muriel raised clear, grave eyes, trying her best to smile.

'You're so good,' she said tremulously. 'I don't know what to say, how to thank you.'

'When you and I give to each other, Muriel, there's no need for thanks.'

'But you are doing all the giving; I have nothing to give in return.'

'Your love ... and that's everything.' His gaze was infinitely tender; Muriel put her arms round his neck and kissed him softly on the lips.

'It's yours for ever and ever,' she whispered huskily.

'Oh, I'm so happy, and to think – it is all due to Aunt Edith.'

'Yes; and that reminds me, she's just been on the phone.'

'At this time? What for?'

'Wanted to know if I'd proposed to you yet.'

'At this time?' she said again, blinking at him. 'She has to walk nearly a mile to a phone box!'

'Couldn't contain herself, apparently,' he laughed, and then, 'I have a shrewd suspicion that she wants to be the first to tell Christine.'

How would she take it? Muriel wondered, and couldn't help expressing her thoughts to Andrew. He shrugged indifferently.

'I don't think it matters how she takes it,' he said, releasing Muriel as his secretary knocked quietly and entered the office.

'Mr. Pickard has just rung through,' said Miss Cook stiffly after measuring them both with disapproving eyes. 'He said you phoned him first thing and told him you would be bringing Miss Paterson over about twenty to nine.' She glanced at the clock; it was ten minutes past nine. 'He has to go out and wants to know if you're taking her over at once. If not, he'll be back about eleven o'clock.'

'Tell him I'll be over immediately.'

'Miss Cook doesn't like me,' Muriel said as she left the room.

'There are very few people she does like,' Andrew replied with a faint smile. 'She's odd, but worth her weight in gold as a secretary. Come on, darling, you're not scared, are you?'

'Terribly,' she said in a faltering voice. 'I'm sure I won't be able to do it, Andrew.'

But Mr. Pickard, grey-haired, and fatherly in spite

of his rather fierce expression, instantly put her at her ease, and Muriel was soon sitting beside a smiling girl who had been instructed to show her what to do. Every head was raised, and odd glances were directed first at Muriel and then at Andrew. Never before had the managing director himself escorted a new girl to the department!

'All right now?' Andrew smiled down at her, something in the still cool depths of his eyes instilling her with a strange new confidence in herself.

'Yes, thank you, An— Mr. Burke.'

He grinned at her, and after speaking a little while with Mr. Pickard, left the office.

The rest of the morning seemed to fly; at ten past twelve Mr. Pickard called Muriel over to him and handed her a folder.

'Mr. Burke has asked me to send you over to his office with these figures. You know your way?' His face was impassive; whatever his thoughts concerning the telephone message he had just received, he hid them admirably.

'I think so,' Muriel replied doubtfully, remembering the maze of corridors through which Andrew had brought her. 'I turn to the left when I leave here?'

'Yes; then straight on, through the main offices, then turn left again.'

Finding herself almost running along the corridor, Muriel slackened her pace, flushing self-consciously as she realized she couldn't get to Andrew quickly enough. Her heart was fluttering as, after knocking on the door and waiting for his 'Come in', she placed the folder before him.

'The figures you sent for,' she said, trying to sound businesslike and brisk.

'What an efficient little puss you look!' laughed

Andrew, his gaze passing from the neat black skirt to the crisp white blouse and then to the hair fixed firmly back with a little bow in the nape of her neck. 'Rather too efficient. Untie your hair.'

'Untie it?'

'For the time being; I'm taking you out to lunch.'

'Oh, lovely!' she exclaimed impulsively, and then blushed. 'I mean, thank you very much.'

'Where's your coat?'

'In a cloakroom round there.' Muriel pointed vaguely towards the outer office. 'Miss Cook told me to put it there.'

'Run along and get it, then; I'll wait here.'

He was ready when she returned, and as they walked the short distance to the restaurant where Andrew always took his lunch, he asked about her new job.

'I like it very much. I felt as though I was a real nuisance to Miss Stevens, but she didn't seem to mind how many questions I asked.'

'I'm glad you're liking it.' He smiled quizzically down at her. 'I hope you're not feeling sorry to be leaving it so soon'

'No ... but I'll be lonely while you're away at the office. What on earth shall I find to do?'

They had reached the restaurant; Andrew took her arm as they crossed to a small table in the corner.

'I could give you an answer that would produce one of your very adorable blushes,' he said quietly. 'But I prefer to wait until we're quite alone.'

'You appear to have given me an answer,' Muriel returned as she sat down, 'and I'm not blushing!'

'That's what you think, my dear.' He passed her the menu. 'Grapefruit?'

'Yes, please.'

During the meal Andrew fell strangely silent, and at

times, a worried frown would appear on his brow. At last Muriel said anxiously,

'Is anything wrong, Andrew?'

'Wrong?'

'You seem to be – sort of – troubled.'

He sighed, hesitating before he answered her.

'I had a talk to my mother last night. I told her I was to be married, and she – she—'

'She didn't like the idea?' The words came slowly, reluctantly, in a tone of deep uneasiness. Her happiness could not be complete if she were to be the cause of a rift between Andrew and his mother. From little things he had said on the cruise, Muriel knew he was devoted to her.

'No, darling, it isn't that,' he reassured her hastily. 'She's a little anxious, naturally, until she meets you . . . but she's been telling me for years that I ought to be married. It's the house—' Again he hesitated. 'Muriel, dear, I know it's only reasonable that you should expect a house of your own – in fact, Mother thinks so too, but—'

Muriel finished quietly,

'—you don't want your mother to leave her home.'

'I think – I think I prefer to buy a house for us.'

'But you're not happy at the thought of leaving *your* home?' Muriel said gently. 'You once told me you were born there, and your father. And you told me about the lovely trees your grandfather had planted.'

'It isn't important; the important thing is that you are happy, and it scarcely ever works out if two women—'

'Dearest Andrew, you banished all my worries so very simply this morning, remember?' She smiled lovingly at him. 'Now I can banish yours just as simply. I don't mind in the least living with your mother.'

'You... darling!' The troubled lines vanished from his brow, but he added anxiously, 'Are you sure? – quite, quite sure?'

'If she's half as sweet as you, I shall love being with her.'

Reaching across the table, Andrew covered her hand with his own.

'I shall always remember this,' he said. 'It's a sacrifice and I—'

'No, no, it's not,' she began, when he interrupted her.

'It *is* a sacrifice for a woman not to have a house of her very own, not to surround herself with the things of her own choosing.' He smiled faintly. 'I may be a mere man, but I know a little about a woman's feelings, her incurable sentimentality, if only from watching my mother dusting certain things with her best handkerchief.'

'Does she do that?' Muriel exclaimed impulsively. 'Oh, I know I shall love her!'

'Why, do you do that?'

'Yes.' She did not add that the little china dog Andrew had bought her on the ship was the only object that came in for this special favour.

'Yes, I think you'll grow to love Mother,' Andrew said with confidence, after a thoughtful pause. 'And there's no doubt at all that she will love you. And, in time, I think you will love the house. When can I take you home?' he added with almost boyish eagerness. 'Tonight?'

'Not tonight, Andrew,' she said apologetically. 'I promised Dil I would go and see her – I did tell you about her baby, didn't I?'

'You talked about nothing else for the latter part of the journey last night,' was Andrew's dry rejoinder.

'And there were so many much more important things I wanted to talk about.'

'Well, it's nice being an aunt; it gives one a feeling of importance. And it's such a dear little thing.'

'You would have been an aunt very soon in any case. My elder sister, Sally, has a boy of four. But I hardly think, when you know him, that you'll call him a "dear little thing"; he's the most mischievous rascal that ever lived.'

'Oh, but he's just at that age,' Muriel retorted, in defence of this unknown nephew-to-be. 'You have to make excuses.'

'Well, I'm afraid I don't,' said Andrew grimly. 'I find his visits much more endurable when I've spanked some obedience into him.'

'You should never, never hit children,' Muriel returned knowledgeably. 'All the books and all the newspaper articles tell you that.'

'Have *you* been reading about child psychology?' he asked with amused interest.

'Dil had several books lent to her, and I read them. One in particular is extremely good; I've promised to buy it for her.'

'Don't,' was Andrew's prompt advice. 'Buy her a tickler instead, she'll find it far more effective. Eve wouldn't be without hers for anything.'

'A tickler?' Muriel stared blankly. 'What's that?'

'You don't know?' Andrew looked at her with mock astonishment. 'A tickler is a cane with a bunch of feathers on one end. They're just a blind of course; for what self-respecting housewife tickles the dust instead of removing it?'

'You mean—? Andrew, you're teasing me!'

'Not at all, darling. That's what ticklers are made for. No parent should be without one. We shall have to get one some day; Mother's is probably worn out – there were three of us, you see.'

'Indeed we shall not! You're teasing me; I don't believe your mother ever even touched you with a – a tickler!'

'Then ask her for yourself. Which brings me back to the question; when are you coming home with me?'

Although rather scared of meeting Mrs. Burke, Muriel suggested that she should go home with him the following evening straight from work.

'You see, if I went home first it would make it very late.'

'Yes, of course, there's no sense in your going home first, but—' He paused. 'I have to go to Sheffield in the morning, and it will be at least three o'clock before I get back, so I think I'll make a day of it – I'll take a couple of hours off. You can do the same; I'll call back at the office for you.'

'*I* take a couple of hours off, so soon? What will Mr. Pickard say?'

'I don't think he'll raise any objections,' Andrew replied with some amusement, adding, 'Not if I ask him nicely.'

'Won't he . . . think something?'

'He'll know something shortly when our engagement is announced. Mother would want that,' he added. 'You don't mind?'

'N-no. . . .' Recalling her own anguish at the idea of reading the announcement of Andrew's engagement to Christine, Muriel felt, even though she now disliked her cousin excessively, that she wanted to spare her as much as possible. 'I don't suppose it makes any difference,' she said, almost to herself.

Although guessing at her thoughts, Andrew made no comment.

'I've been thinking, darling, as tomorrow is Friday, there seems no reason why you shouldn't stay with us for the week-end ... or perhaps your mother would object? After all, she doesn't know me.'

Muriel felt sure her mother would not object, but she would make no promise until she had asked her permission.

'I'll see what she says and let you know tomorrow.' She paused, thinking of the small house with its drab furniture and faded curtains; trying to visualize Andrew's home and compare the two. 'Andrew. . . .'

'Sweetheart?'

'You will come to my home, won't you?'

'But of course, darling, just as soon as you like.'

'It's only a small house, in a row—' She was checked by the rebuke in his eyes.

'I hope I've never given you reason to think me a snob, Muriel.' It was the curt, rather arrogant tone he had used more than once on the ship. A tone that seemed to belie his own words; a tone she did not like to hear.

'I'm sorry ... I was only trying to tell you— Don't be cross, Andrew.' Would she always be so abominably hurt by a mere change of tone? It was a frightening thought.

The pleading had its effect; Andrew's face softened instantly, bringing back the happy glow to her eyes; convincing her that he would never be angry with her for very long.

It was arranged that Andrew should visit Muriel's home the following week, after Muriel had ascertained which evening would be convenient to her mother. Then Andrew brought up the question of an engagement ring.

'You shall choose it,' Muriel told him. 'I know I

shall like what you like.'

But Andrew shook his head.

'A friend of mine did that ... and his choice did *not* happen to agree with that of his fiancée; with the result that, now they're married, she never wears it. That's not going to happen with us. You're having all your own way in this.' There was the merest hesitation before the last two words, and because she noticed it, Muriel said banteringly,

'Does that mean that I'm always going to have my own way ... in everything?'

'No, my dear, it does not ... and you knew it before you asked the question.'

'Nevertheless,' she said, with a candour that was soon to become incurable where Andrew was concerned, 'I liked the answer.'

'I'm profoundly relieved to hear it.'

'No, you're not!' came the quick retort. 'It wouldn't make the slightest difference whether I liked the answer or not.'

'No, quite honestly, my pet, it wouldn't.' And, after glancing at his watch, 'If we don't move you're going to receive a severe ticking off.'

Gathering up her handbag and gloves, Muriel rose hastily. 'Will I be late?' she asked anxiously.

'A little, I'm afraid.'

'Oh, dear— What will Mr. Pickard say?'

'Well,' began Andrew teasingly, 'you will first receive a reproving glance, and then a frigid, "You do not appear to know that we have one hour only for lunch, Miss Paterson. Take five hundred lines".'

'Stupid!' she laughed. 'No, really, what will he say?'

'Nothing – the people in that department are allowed ten minutes or so, both morning and lunchtime.'

'Just in that department? But why?'

'At certain times of the year they have to put in a good deal of overtime; and in return we make them this small concession.'

What a lot she was learning about him, Muriel mused as she trotted to keep up with the pace that always appeared to be unhurried. Only this time yesterday – was it only yesterday? – she had known so little. She had not thought him capable of such infinite tenderness, of such consideration for his staff.

'Are you coming over for a few minutes before you go home?' Andrew was saying. 'I must have a good-night kiss to see me over till tomorrow afternoon.'

'I . . . well, all right, then.'

'That doesn't sound very enthusiastic,' he frowned.

'I wanted to see – er – Peter,' she told him hesitantly.

'Peter?' Andrew's frown deepened.

'Peter Thomson – you remember, the young man who – who—'

'Ah, yes, the young man who was *not* making love to you.' His brow cleared. 'You want to tell him?'

'Yes, please, Andrew. I do want to tell him myself. You don't mind?'

'No, but I intend to have my kiss. I'll send over for some more figures at ten to five.'

Peter hid his feelings admirably, and after the first shock of surprise offered Muriel sincere congratulations and wishes for her future happiness. Nevertheless, she knew he was hurt, and she was feeling far from happy as she entered her sister's ward at the hospital. Dil's first words, however, drove all thoughts of Peter from her mind for the moment.

'You're a dark horse! Getting married next month and not a word to anyone!'

'How – how do you know?' Muriel stared at her in astonishment.

'Aunt Edith has been to see Mother this morning; she was on her way to Aunt Sarah's. Why didn't you tell Mother last night— Oh, yes, I know he proposed to you last night. Aunt Edith rang him up this morning.'

'Aunt Edith was going to see Aunt Sarah? ... It was only to tell Christine about our engagement. Oh, she's dreadful!'

'Why? She's got to know some time.' Dil chuckled. 'Aunt Edith said that as she did all the work she was taking good care she had her reward. Gosh, I envy her! I'd give a lot to see Christine's face when she hears the news. Imagine little you grabbing her bloke – she'll never forgive you—'

'Stop it, Dil! I hate your talking like this.' Muriel's eyes glinted angrily as she sat down by the bed.

'Sorry.' Dil took her hand. 'I didn't mean that about grabbing. I know everything, and it's pretty obvious that you've been through it since you parted at the end of the cruise. It's obvious, too, that you confided in Aunt Edith because you felt you had to tell someone. I hate myself for everything I've said to you. *I* should have been the one in whom you could have confided. I'm sorry, Muriel, and I'm glad that you're going to be happy.'

There was no doubting her sincerity. This was a new Dil, the sister Muriel had always longed for ... a real sister. Muriel felt she was going to cry.

'Thank you, Dil ... oh, I'm s-so h-happy. ...'

Seeing the tears, Dil said briskly,

'Well, if this is how you look when you're happy, heaven forbid that I shall ever see you in the depths of despair!' And the tears turned to laughter.

'I know I'm stupid; but everyone is so kind. Andrew—' Muriel drew an audible breath. 'Dil, he's wonderful!'

'I knew he must be something exceptional,' Dil returned with a grin, 'when Christine wanted him.' She paused, becoming serious. 'Why didn't you tell Mother last night?'

'She told me you'd found a house, and I thought we wouldn't be able to be married for a long time. I wanted to talk to Andrew about it first.'

'What did he say?' Dil looked at her curiously.

'He said he would make it possible for me to allow Mother something.'

'Couldn't wait, eh? He sounds a pet. When's the wedding?'

'We haven't fixed the date yet.'

'You realize you'll have to invite our charming cousin?'

'No.' Muriel shook her head. 'I couldn't do that.'

'But you'll also have to leave out Aunt Sarah and Uncle Herbert.'

'Oh, dear, yes. And Andrew is a business friend of Uncle Herbert's.' Muriel looked worried. 'I suppose we shall have to invite them all – but Christine won't come,' she added with conviction.

'I rather think she will, if only to save her face. She won't want you to know she's feeling vindictive.'

'I know already,' said Muriel, and went on to tell her sister of Christine's threat. 'Of course,' she added, 'Christine didn't know that Aunt Edith had already told Andrew; neither did I, that's why I agreed to leave the factory.'

The deep, angry colour had slowly fused Dil's cheeks as her sister was speaking, but her voice was more perturbed than angry as she said,

'You're sure, Muriel, quite sure, that Aunt Edith told him everything? She says she did, but you don't think she may have glossed it over a bit?'

'I think she would tell Andrew in a different way from what Christine would have done, but she told him everything,' Muriel answered, realizing that her heart was suddenly fluttering strangely. 'Why – why are you looking like that, Dil? Christine can't do me any harm now.'

'I don't know. . . .' Dil fell silent for a moment. 'I'd rather trust a viper than Christine. Are you sure Andrew knows the whole of it?' she asked again. 'That he knows you went on the cruise hoping to find a rich—?'

'Yes, yes,' Muriel interrupted hastily. 'And he's overlooked it all— Dil, you're frightening me!'

'I'm sorry; but I have such a queer feeling inside me. . . . Christine's poison, and after what you've told me I can't see her letting this wedding go on without doing something to stop it.'

'But what can she do? Christine can only tell Andrew what he already knows – that is supposing he would listen to her, and he won't. He said she would get more than she bargains for if she goes tale-carrying to him,' but her voice was shaking in spite of its confidence.

'He thinks she may go to see him?' Regretting having upset Muriel, Dil's one desire was to reassure her.

'Yes.'

'Oh, well, in that case, there's nothing to worry about.'

But Muriel was far from being reassured. On the contrary, she had an inexplicable feeling of guilt, a subconscious conviction that she had committed some crime of which Andrew was in total ignorance. It was ridiculous, she told herself. There was nothing ... *nothing*. ...

CHAPTER TWELVE

ALL the next morning Muriel was filled with uneasiness without knowing why. Over and over again she kept telling herself that her cousin could not possibly harm her, but when, at half-past three, Mr. Pickard told her that Andrew was now in his office and that she might go, she found herself trembling as she began to tidy up her desk. And there was no running along the corridor this time; her legs felt so weak that they could collapse under her at any moment.

Andrew was standing by the desk, his powerful form appearing more massive than ever in the thick grey overcoat. Frantically Muriel scanned his face; the jaw looked more square, the eyes more stern—

'Hello, precious.' No sternness in his eyes now; they smiled at her and his arms were outstretched invitingly.

'Andrew!' How she covered the distance between them she never knew, but she was in his arms, her cheek resting against the rough tweed of his coat. 'Andrew. ...' At the choked little sob of relief, Andrew held her away from him, examining her face critically.

'Are you feeling all right?'

'Yes, wonderful,' but she snuggled to him again, as though for safety. 'Please let me stay like this for a little while.'

He held her closely until her trembling was stilled.

'Now, what is it?' he asked gently. 'What has upset you, my darling?'

'I thought – I thought— Did Christine come and see you last night?'

'No.' He looked puzzled. 'What difference could it make if she had?'

'She might have managed to convince you that I was – wicked, I mean, if she'd given you her version of the story—'

'Is that all that's worrying you?' he interrupted, shaking her slightly. 'You are a little idiot, Muriel. Christine won't be given the chance to say one single word against you. If she has the impudence to come to me she'll receive the telling off of her life and then be shown the door. When did this stupid notion occur to you?'

'Last night.'

'And I suppose,' he observed sternly, 'you've had no sleep?'

'Not very much,' she admitted, feeling rather foolish at having worried so unnecessarily.

'For that you'll go to bed early tonight— You are staying?'

'Yes; Mother didn't mind at all.'

An hour later she was being introduced to Andrew's mother. She was just as Muriel had imagined her, tall and dark, with her son's aristocratic bearing. She looked at Muriel critically, from head to toe, and Muriel found herself searching vaguely for the words of a song her grandmother used to sing. All she could remember was, 'poor John' and a sudden, irrepressible smile of amusement broke, dispelling her nervousness and bringing an unexpected twinkle to Mrs. Burke's eyes. It was almost as though she read Muriel's thoughts.

'We all have to go through this, my dear; a son is a very precious possession to have to give to another woman. But Andrew always had such excellent taste; you're approved.'

'Thank you,' returned Muriel, still smiling, but with an inward sigh of relief.

'Where's Betty?' inquired Andrew, suddenly looking grim. 'Not home from school yet? I suppose she's loitering about with that boy-friend of hers again!'

'Now, dear, please don't be old-fashioned. He's a very nice boy. Why should you mind if he carries her satchel home for her?'

'I don't – it's the time it takes. Where on earth can they get to?'

'Betty is nearly fifteen,' Mrs. Burke remined him. 'Surely she can be trusted?'

'If you knew one half the things she says to me, you most certainly wouldn't trust her.' He took Muriel's arm. 'Come into the drawing-room, Muriel. Tea will be ready in a few minutes.'

All through tea he was uneasy, continually glancing at the clock; when it was over he went to the front door.

'There's a mist coming up,' he said, with a mixture of anger and anxiety. 'Unless I'm mistaken, it will be thick before very long.'

He waited a few more minutes, then went to the door again.

'It's thicker already,' he said. 'I'll have to go out and look for her.'

It was nearly six o'clock; Mrs. Burke's face was becoming harassed, too.

'This has never happened before—'

'No, and it won't happen again,' Andrew cut her short grimly. 'I shall see to that!' And, turning to Muriel, 'I'm sorry, dear, but I must go. You don't mind?'

178

'Of course not. Would you like me to come with you?'

'No; it's bitterly cold, there's no sense in your coming out.'

Muriel sat with Mrs. Burke, neither of them speaking for a long while. But at last Muriel said soothingly,

'Don't worry, Mrs. Burke, I'm sure Andrew will find her before very long.'

'But she can't be lost— Something dreadful must have happened to her!'

'No . . . don't upset yourself. My brother has had us all in this state, many times, but he's always turned up safe and sound.'

Mrs. Burke was shaking her head, and a moment later she rose agitatedly.

'I'll have to go out myself; I can't sit here doing nothing. You must excuse me, Muriel.' She was gone before Muriel could offer to accompany her.

Five minutes elapsed; it seemed like an eternity. Feeling that she, too, could sit still no longer, Muriel went to the front door. As she opened it the fog choked her and she was just about to close it again when a car pulled up with a screeching of brakes and a muttered exclamation from the driver. Then Muriel recognized the voice of her uncle's chauffeur.

'We should never have come; I don't know how we're to get back—'

'Stop grumbling, Hooper, I've told you I'll only be five minutes!' Christine, muffled in furs, was already at the door. 'You . . . !' She stared at Muriel with hatred, but there was also an expression of triumph in her eyes and Muriel found herself trembling as she stepped aside for her to enter the house.

'Why have you come here, Christine? If it's to see Andrew, I must tell you that he won't listen—'

'Where is he?' Christine cut in imperiously. 'Tell him I want to see him!'

'He's not in at the moment—'

'Then I'll wait.'

'Very well.' With a little shrug Muriel led the way into the sitting-room. 'Won't you sit down?'

'Quite the hostess, aren't you?' Christine sneered. 'Where's Mrs. Burke?'

'She and Andrew are both looking for Betty; she's out somewhere in the fog.'

'Is this your first visit here?' and when Muriel nodded, 'Came to meet the future mother-in-law, eh? Did she approve?'

'I think so.'

'How sad. Everything going so splendidly for you, and I have to come and spoil it all.' Christine sighed mockingly and moved over to the fire.

'Andrew knows all there is to know about me,' Muriel said quietly, 'and he has forgiven it.'

'Because that meddling old busybody made excuses for you. She did it to spite me, because she's always disliked me!' Christine had raised her voice, but it dropped again to a malevolent softness as she continued, 'but she has apparently been left in ignorance of one thing ... and you've forgotten it. I said nothing the other night because I thought I'd destroyed it—'

'What are you talking about?' Muriel's voice was sharp, because a terrible fear was creeping over her. 'I've told you, Andrew knows everything.'

'Not quite everything, my sweet, innocent little cousin.' Opening her handbag, Christine withdrew a letter and waved it triumphantly in Muriel's face. 'So he's forgiven you, has he? Do you suppose he'll be so ready to forgive this?'

'It's the letter I sent on the cruise.' Muriel looked blank. 'There's nothing in that.'

'We shall see if *he* treats it so lightly—' She broke off, looking at Muriel with puzzlement. 'Have you forgotten what you wrote?'

'I remember every word.' Muriel's bewilderment increased. The letter told only of her love for Andrew, describing him in flowery terms that would doubtless afford him considerable amusement, but nothing more. 'Do you really imagine that letter can harm me? I think you must be out of your mind!' She moved away, but still faced her cousin across the room. 'Don't you think you're being very foolish, Christine? That letter is useless to you, and you will only make a complete fool of yourself by giving it to Andrew.' What had come over Christine? Muriel wondered. It was incredible that she should suppose that the letter would turn Andrew against her.

'It seems to me,' said Christine, moving towards her, 'that your memory needs refreshing. I shall read the letter to you – at least, certain parts of it.' The unmistakable note of triumph in her voice; the way she drew the letter from its envelope, as though wishing to keep her cousin in suspense, to torture her slowly, caused Muriel's face to whiten and her throat to contract. She put a trembling hand to her breast, feeling the violent thumping of her heart, and moved further back until the heavy velvet curtains touched her legs.

A terrible suspicion was beginning to creep over her.

'You talk first of your meeting with Andrew as the greatest piece of luck that's ever come your way,' Christine said, and went on – 'I never thought it could be so simple, and I must admit that at first I didn't intend trying my luck on him because I didn't like him very much. However, when I saw he was attracted to me I thought it would be foolish to waste the opportunity, as he's very rich indeed.' She paused, smiling as Muriel put her hands to her ears. 'I was going to ask if you wanted any more, but it appears that you don't.'

'I didn't mean to send that letter,' Muriel managed to say at last through whitened lips. 'I wrote another, telling you I loved him – Aunt Edith mixed them, and the wrong one was posted.'

'Not very original,' Christine laughed, 'even though you had only a moment in which to invent it. No, my dear Muriel, it won't serve. I told you the other night that if I couldn't have Andrew, you would not have him either. You wrote this letter, and he shall read it. You've played on his pity; persuaded Aunt Edith to paint you as a little innocent – heartbroken – but now he shall judge for himself.'

'I didn't know of Aunt Edith's intentions,' Muriel denied. 'And I never played on his pity. I was forced to take work at the factory.' She paused. 'I suppose it's no use reminding you that Andrew will be hurt, as well, by this?'

'Not a bit—' Christine turned expectantly, but it was a maid who entered the room.

'Excuse me, miss, but your chauffeur wishes to speak to you.'

Christine's lips compressed; she muttered something impatiently under her breath.

'I'll come immediately. Is the fog worse?'

'It's very bad, miss. Your chauffeur says it isn't safe to drive in.'

'Fetch me an envelope, will you?' Christine requested after a thoughtful pause. Then she left the room.

When she returned the envelope was on the table.

Muriel watched in frightened fascination as her cousin addressed it. The letter was put inside, the envelope sealed and stamped.

'If I post it here in the village Andrew should get it by the first post tomorrow.' At the door Christine turned, laughing. 'Good night, Muriel . . . and pleasant dreams. . . .'

She was shivering, and moved slowly to the fire. This was the end of her dreams; her engagement had lasted less than forty-eight hours—

No, not less, for she would have tonight. For a little while longer she would have Andrew's love, feel his tenderness, see his lips soften when he smiled at her. And surely there would be at least one kiss.

There was a slight haze about the room, as though the fog crept in somewhere. It must be very thick indeed, Muriel thought, feeling suddenly afraid for Andrew's safety. She had just decided to go to the door again when Mrs. Burke came in.

'Isn't Andrew back yet?' she asked in dismay. 'Oh, where can Betty have got to?'

'Do sit down,' Muriel urged, pulling a chair closer to the fire. 'You're perished.'

'I can't—' She turned. 'Andrew! So you haven't found her?'

'It's all right, Mother; she's staying the night at Sally's.' Andrew walked across the room and, pulling aside the curtains, closed the window. Then, turning, he looked steadily at Muriel until she was forced to lower her eyes.

'How do you know?' Mrs. Burke had sunk into the chair with a sigh of profound relief. 'You haven't had time to go there.'

'The telephone was ringing as I came in; Betty and this boy-friend of hers took the road by the common, and as you know, the fog always settles there first. Betty decided to make for Sally's, but apparently they had some difficulty in finding the house, for they've only just arrived. Sally rang immediately.'

'Thank God! Is the boy staying, too?'

'No; he had already gone when Sally phoned.' His voice was harsh, and it seemed to Muriel that he tried desperately to suppress an inner fury. Fortunate that Betty was staying the night with her sister, Muriel mused, hoping his anger would soon subside. It would be more than she could bear if he remained like this for the whole of their last evening together.

All through dinner his face retained its harsh expression, and each time Muriel caught his glance she felt that her very soul was being pierced. Later, all having returned to the sitting-room, Mrs. Burke told Muriel of Andrew's wonderful collection of gramophone records, and invited her to play some of her own choosing.

'This is my very special favourite,' Muriel said, waiting for the needle to come down on Tchaikowsky's *Walzer Aus Der Serenade*'. Andrew listened for a few seconds, then rose abruptly.

'You must excuse me, Mother, I have some work to do,' he said, and left the room without even a glance at Muriel.

'Well!' Mrs. Burke stared at the closed door. 'And his favourite record, too! You must excuse him, dear,' she said, turning apologetically to Muriel. 'It must be something at the works – he's always like this when anything goes wrong; shuts himself up in his study until the problem is solved. It's one of the things you'll have to get used to, my dear. He'll be as right as rain in the morning.'

'In the morning!' Muriel exclaimed in dismay.

'Won't he come back again tonight?' She could not understand him; he had been so anxious to be with her. They had a nice long week-end in which to make up some of the time they had lost, he told her driving down in the car . . . and yet he had left the room without even an apology, without even a glance. . . .

'I shall go and fetch him,' Mrs. Burke said with a touch of anger. 'He has no right to leave you on your first evening – I can't understand it at all. He has all day tomorrow to grapple with his problems.'

Was it something to do with work? Muriel wondered, feeling sure that Betty could not be to blame for Andrew's conduct. But he had not said anything to Muriel about any problems at work.

'Do you mind if I go?' she asked hesitantly.

'Of course not, dear. It's the room opposite to this.'

After knocking quietly Muriel waited for Andrew's 'Come in' before entering his study. He was standing by the fire, but turned as she entered.

'What is it, Muriel? I don't want to be interrupted!'

Muriel was so taken aback by the sharpness of his tone that for a moment she was unable to speak.

'I'm sorry, but it was just that. . . .'

'Just what?'

'Nothing.' She stared at him miserably.

'You must have had some reason for coming. What is it?'

After a slight hesitation Muriel moved over to him.

'Do you have to work tonight, Andrew?'

'Yes.'

'Then – then I won't disturb you.' She managed to smile. 'But may I come back later, to say good night?'

'If you like.'

'I do hope you solve your problem,' she said, turning to smile at him again before going out.

The rest of the evening dragged unbearably. Several times Mrs. Burke, looking most uncomfortable, announced her intention of bringing Andrew back, but Muriel stopped her, saying she was quite happy playing her favourite records. She waited till half-past ten, then replaced all the records in the cabinet.

'Are you going to bed now, dear?' Mrs. Burke spoke with obvious relief.

'Yes, when I've said good night to Andrew.' She bade Mrs. Burke good night and went across to Andrew's room.

He was sitting by the fire, staring into the flames. No sign that he had been working, no books or papers on the desk.

'Have you finished?' Muriel walked over to him, and stood looking down. 'Your mother said you had a problem; is it solved to your satisfaction?'

A smile curved Andrew's lips.

'Yes, dear, my – problem is solved.' Reaching for her hand, he drew her down on to his knee.

'I'm glad,' she said, finding a resting place for her head. 'May I stay for a little while?'

'Of course you may. What's the matter, darling?'

'Nothing – now that you're nice to me again. Was Betty the cause of your crossness, or was it the problem?'

'It was the problem,' he replied, in an odd tone.

'Was it very difficult?'

'Not after I'd thought about it for a little while.'

Although feeling that she should show interest, Muriel could not waste precious moments talking about his work.

'I missed you horribly; I wanted to be with you tonight – more than anything tonight,' she said, a catch in her voice.

'There'll be other nights – thousands of them.'

Little he knew, she thought, that there would be no more nights, that tomorrow morning he would be hating her, both for what she was, and for the pain she was causing him.

'I love you,' she whispered desperately. 'I do love you— Please believe that!'

'I do believe it,' Andrew responded gravely. 'Otherwise my problem wouldn't have been solved so easily.'

Muriel leant away, her face bewildered.

'What has my love to do with your work?'

Andrew ignored that.

'I solved my problem by asking two very simple questions,' he said. ' "Does she love me?" and "Can I live without her?" The answer to the first was yes, and to the second, no. After that everything was clear. The letter shall be burnt ... unopened.'

'Andrew!' Muriel sprang up, the colour leaving her face. 'You know there's a letter in the post?'

'The window was open,' he said quietly. 'I came round by the orchard....'

The colour flooded back into Muriel's face; she moved further away from his chair.

'Did you hear Christine reading – reading—' Her throat went dry and she could not go on.

'Yes, Muriel; I heard Christine reading extracts from the letter.'

'And yet you still—? But you can't! You *must* hate me! No decent girl writes a letter like that. What did you *think* when you heard?'

'I could have strangled you,' Andrew admitted. 'But something far stronger than my temper urged me to think things over calmly before I did anything I'd regret – the same thing has happened before, and some day I shall tell you about it,' he added, and went on,

'That was why I came in here. I pictured what would happen if I allowed my anger to have its sway; the scene between us, in which I would say things I'd regret almost immediately, your going away, perhaps a long way away. I pictured my anxiety, more wasted time, before I found you – and I would have found you, my darling, for I know I can never be happy without you. It all seemed so stupid and unnecessary, because I was already asking myself those two questions and knowing the answers.'

Muriel was almost in tears.

'You can't love me now you've heard what I wrote – you can't!'

He held out a hand to her.

'Come over here and I'll show you whether I love you or not.'

Muriel turned her back on him, hanging her head.

'I'm too ashamed.'

'Then I shall come to you.' His hands were on her shoulders, gently bringing her round to face him. 'We both did things on that cruise for which we've since been ashamed, but it's all in the past. The future is ours.' He kissed her lips and held her quietly for a little while, then drew her over to the fire, putting a cushion at his feet. 'Sit down, darling.'

Muriel sat down, resting her head against his knees.

'I don't deserve this; I was detestable—'

'I thought, sweetheart, that we were forgetting the past,' Andrew said, but added, 'I'm glad we both went on the cruise, but don't ask me to go on another for a long, long time, will you? It would only revive the memory of my detestable conduct.'

'I'll *never* ask you to go on a cruise,' was Muriel's fervent reply.

Ten minutes later Mrs. Burke came in to bid

Andrew good night.

'Don't stay up too long,' she added, turning to the door. 'I'm sure Muriel is tired.'

'We're going up at once,' Andrew said. 'We've been discussing our honeymoon, but haven't been able to make a decision.' He smiled affectionately at her. 'Have you any suggestions?'

'But of course,' she replied, trying to be helpful. 'What could be more romantic than a cruise—? Surely you've not forgotten where you met?'

Mills & Boon
Best Seller Romances

The very best of Mills & Boon Romances
brought back for those of you who missed
them when they were first published.
In January
we bring back the following four
great romantic titles.

STARS OF SPRING
by Anne Hampson

When Joanne inherited a farm in the lovely Douro district of
Portugal, it seemed the answer to a problem, as she now had
five-year-old Glee to look after. The only fly in the ointment was
that the farm was on the estate of Dom Manoel Alvares – and he
wanted it himself!

RACHEL TREVELLYAN
by Anne Mather

The arrogant Luis Martinez, Marques de Mendao, made it clear that
all he felt for Rachel was contempt. Did it matter that she seemed
unable to convince him that he was wrong about her? And what
about Malcolm's feelings?

VALLEY OF PARADISE
by Margaret Rome

Serena was almost desperate when she answered an advertisement
that offered 'lifelong security' to the successful applicant. It was a
move that was to take her to far-off Chile, to a husband she had
never met – and to what else?

THE DEVIL'S DARLING
by Violet Winspear

'But you don't know me – you don't love me,' Persepha protested
when the magnetic Don Diablo Ezreldo Ruy announced his intention
of marrying her. 'In Mexico, *señorita*, the knowing and the loving
come after marriage,' he told her. But would they?

If you have difficulty in obtaining any of these books through
your local paperback retailer, write to:
Mills & Boon Reader Service
P.O. Box 236, Thornton Road, Croydon, Surrey, CR9 3RU

Mills & Boon
Best Seller Romances

The very best of Mills & Boon
brought back for those of you
who missed reading them when they
were first published.
There are three other Best Seller Romances
for you to collect this month.

LAND OF ENCHANTMENT
by Janet Dailey

Diana was a city girl, a glamorous model; Lije Masters was a tough rancher from New Mexico. But they met, fell in love, and were married – just like that. Would Diana now find herself 'repenting at leisure'?

COME THE VINTAGE
by Anne Mather

Ryan's father had left her a half share of his prosperous vine-growing business, and the other half to a man she had never heard of, a Frenchman named Alain de Beaunes – on condition that they married each other. So, for the sake of the business, they married, neither caring anything for the other. Where did they go from there?

COURT OF THE VEILS
by Violet Winspear

'In many respects the desert is like a woman. Anything might crop up in the desert, as in a relationship with a woman... But a man can enjoy the desert without getting involved – emotionally.' Duane Hunter's words made it quite plain to Roslyn that there was no future for her in his life. And yet...

If you have difficulty in obtaining any of these books through your local paperback retailer, write to:
Mills & Boon Reader Service
P.O. Box 236, Thornton Road, Croydon, Surrey, CR9 3RU

One of the best things in life is... FREE

We're sure you have enjoyed this Mills & Boon romance. So we'd like you to know about the other titles we offer. A world of variety in romance. From the best authors in the world of romance.

The Mills & Boon Reader Service Catalogue lists all the romances that are currently in stock. So if there are any titles that you cannot obtain or have missed in the past, you can get the romances you want DELIVERED DIRECT to your home.

The Reader Service Catalogue is free. Simply send the coupon – or drop us a line asking for the catalogue.

Post to: Mills & Boon Reader Service, P.O. Box 236, Thornton Road, Croydon, Surrey CR9 3RU, England.
*Please note: READERS IN SOUTH AFRICA please write to: Mills & Boon Reader Service of Southern Africa, Private Bag X3010, Randburg 2125, S. Africa.

Please send me my FREE copy of the Mills & Boon Reader Service Catalogue.

NAME (Mrs/Miss) _____ EP1
ADDRESS _____

COUNTY/COUNTRY _____ POST/ZIP CODE _____
BLOCK LETTERS, PLEASE

Mills & Boon
the rose of romance